THE UMBRELLAS
OF HAMELIN

THE UMBRELLAS OF HAMELIN

Written by

Sue Knight

First Published in 2023 by Fantastic Books Publishing
Cover image by Bea Burchill
Cover design by Gabi

ISBN (ebook): 978-1-914060-56-4
ISBN (paperback): 978-1-914060-55-7

To my siblings; Danuta, Penny and John; and to Elizabeth, Kathryn, the two Janets, Jennifer, Mary Jane, and all who shared Disraeli Crescent days.

Acknowledgements

With thanks to the founder of the Thursday Writers Group, Penny, and our fellow member, Danuta, where all this started. And many thanks to Col, for his constant technical help and support.

Contents

The Umbrellas of Hamelin

Anonymous figures trudged across the white gallery wall, heads down, facing the storm; waterproofed bundles moving from right to left – an endless wave of faceless people, each with their grey mac and black umbrella.

Underneath a sign said simply: VIDEO INSTALLATION.

"Talk about life imitating art! It's a monsoon out there." Anita shook her wet hair, a fading red, darkened by the storm. She was glad to see that at least one of them had made it through the weather. She hadn't wanted to spend this lunch hour alone. "I couldn't have spent another minute in that office. Its hassle hassle hassle all day long. If I couldn't get away at lunchtime..." She was relieved at how normal she sounded, as if this was the usual office whinge. In fact, the politics of it made her feel sick and frightened. Every day of the credit crunch made it worse, and every day made it more and more urgent that she keep this job.

Unqualified fifty year olds were having a tough time of it in the world of work at the moment.

Mary smiled a greeting through a large cheese sandwich.

"You don't know how I envy you Mary, being retired."

Mary smiled again and carried on eating. She usually protested that it was all very well, but trying to manage on a pension was no fun. And then she would say that she didn't know what to do with herself nowadays. Although she did. She ate. And she knitted. But she was lonely. Anita knew that. They all did. Lonely and dull. Lonely because she was dull.

1

Yet somehow in their lunchtime sanctuary, in front of the endless video wall, it didn't matter. It didn't matter that Cath was so abrasive. It didn't matter that Lou wasn't the brightest light on the tree.

It didn't matter that she, Anita, was so awkward, and so faded, so old before her time, in a world that worshipped the young. It didn't matter not knowing what to say here. They only met at lunchtime. The room was darkened, they were eating.

"I wondered if anybody else was going to come. The Gallery is really empty today." Mary was muffled by her large untidy sandwich. "I thought Lou was supposed to be back this week, but she's not turned up yet."

There were usually four of them in the little room – a gloomy unvisited offshoot of the main gallery. Anita, Mary, Lou and Cath, four people with no other friends to lunch with. Installation Art of any kind was new and unpopular in the borough, which was something of an unvisited backwater in itself. At any rate, there had been no change in the installation since Anita discovered the lunchtime haven, and the videoed procession of umbrellas still surged at them, ever onwards through the endless rain, and continued to disappear off the wall bottom left into who knew where.

The beauty of it was that no-one else seemed interested, so they had always been able to find a seat here – a quiet corner – away from the stress and the loneliness of the day – to eat their lunch in peace.

Mary stopped eating for a moment and said, "There was some colour this morning, just before you came in." She said it in her usual placid way and carried on eating.

"Colour!" Anita wished that Lou were here. Lou would

have made an occasion out of it. She would have rushed over to tell Anita as soon as she arrived. It would have been such an event in Lou's life. And she herself needed a bit of an occasion today, a feeling that she had a world of her own to live in, a world that had its own excitements.

"Yes. One of the umbrellas tilted before it disappeared and I saw a bit of a yellow scarf. Bright yellow. Silk I reckon."

Mary and Lou always discussed fabrics as they were Quilters and Knitters. Anita looked at the video wall. It was the same as ever, the same grey figures, the same hopeless sort of trudge across the screen. They didn't pay much attention to it usually.

"I tell you girls, they call it art, but I could take that thing on my mobile phone today, no problem." Cath entered, shaking her umbrella over the tiled floor. She had no respect for cloakroom provisions – and not much for modern art. She gestured dismissively at the installation. "I've never seen such rain!"

"Cath" – Anita was very pleased to see her. She didn't make it every day. Maybe Lou would turn up too and they would be the usual foursome. "There was some colour again."

"No!"

This was more like it. "Yes, Mary says that just before one of the umbrella ladies disappeared off the wall she looked round, and Mary saw a silk scarf or something. Yellow. Silk. She says."

They hadn't really believed Lou that time she told them that the umbrellas had changed just before they all arrived. Lou often got overexcited and got things wrong. But if stolid Mary said so…

"Now", Cath was absorbed, "When did Lou see it change?

3

Only if we can count from then to today, we might be able to work out how long before it repeats."

Mary broke away from the carrot she was crunching. "No. Lou saw a red colour. A red check blouse, just a glimpse under the raincoat. Cotton check. Like that material Sally bought. This was yellow, and definitely silk."

Sally, of the red gingham, was the one who had found the little room in the first place. They had all told Anita at various time how she had invited them all in during a March storm. She had seen them huddled in the porch, or wandering aimlessly by, and waved to them.

The way she had said 'they' never come in here had been reassuring. She had chatted to Mary and Lou about their sewing. She had been particularly taken with the bright silk blouse Lou was working on – said it reminded her of the golden sun of Thailand, where she had lived in her youth. She had founded the lunch group, but had not stuck with it.

Anita wasn't surprised. Why would someone like Sally want to lunch with them every day – any day? She obviously fitted perfectly into the dazzling world outside and had returned to it.

"She said one of the ladies looked up, like she had seen something. You could trust Mary on fabrics, so Anita believed her version of what the vanished Sally had seen.

"He must have told them" – by 'he' Cath meant the artist – "he must have told them that every so often they must look up a bit. That's the 'art' in it I suppose."

"You don't know much about art, but you know what you like Cath."

Cath smiled at Anita. They were the only two who had ever

bothered to look at what was in the rest of the Gallery. But then none of the others were gallery goers.

Anita had met them – including the holidaying Lou – when she had taken refuge from the sudden thunderstorm that heralded the end of a glorious spring. She hadn't realised at first there was anyone else in the room, but they had seemed kind and unsurprised to see her. They had said the usual Nice Weather For Ducks things. If Anita remembered right it was Mary who had said it would be nice for the roses, and tall Cath who had said that she hoped 'they' wouldn't dare to start putting any hosepipe bans in action if this was the kind of summer they were going to get. Lou had been absorbed stitching one of her bright silk scarves.

They all agreed it would be nice to be four again and had a gentle grumbling session about the missing Sally, and all chimed in with their stories of how it was her who had invited them all in here.

Anita hadn't said much at all, but somehow it didn't matter. No-one had minded her quietly eating her yoghurt in the semi-dark, saying nothing. There was plenty of room on the benches. They sat on the back one, and those who bought lots of sandwiches and packages – Mary and Lou – used the bench in front as a table. Anita and her yoghurt took up as little room as they possibly could.

Hitting the bottom of her yoghurt pot brought Anita back to the present to hear Mary saying: "Something really lovely it was, Sally said."

"What was lovely?" that was Cath, looking up from her salad.

"As if the umbrella lady had seen something lovely, I mean. Something just where we can't see it. Off the wall."

Anita and Cath smiled at each other again. 'Off the wall' didn't quite convey what Mary was trying to say. Still, it was as near to a discussion of art as Mary had ever got, so Sally's sighting must have made quite an impression.

For the first time, Anita wondered how long the Installation had been playing. It had accompanied them through the wettest summer on record and now looked set to go on into Autumn, which would begin tomorrow.

Even when she first saw it, on the last day of Spring, it had no air of newness or excitement about it. The staff were not concerned – it had no uniformed protector sitting on a chair. It had no chair. Just the two padded benches, so perfect for their lunch.

"This must have been here for quite a long time now." Anita spoke her thoughts aloud. "I wonder if they will be changing it soon."

They ate a while in silence thinking this over. None of them were happy at the thought of what 'they' might do, but none of them said so. Life had taught them that there was nothing to be done about 'they' and their doings.

"Lou wondered if it really played all night." That was Mary, who was packing all her empty lunch boxes into other empty boxes.

"No. They'll turn it off. They aren't going to waste electricity these days. They always say how broke they are. That collecting box in the foyer!" Cath scorned that. To her, free was free.

"Well, Lou wondered." Mary didn't usually persist in the face of Cath's sharpness. "She did say she was going to pop in one night and find out. She wanted to see the colour again I think."

"Pop in! At night." Anita felt she could be safely amused at this and gave Cath another of their looks. This was a good day – so different from her office life. "It's closed at night."

"She cleans here" said Cath surprised – not returning the look. "She could have popped in any night if she wanted to. If she'd been interested. She's not keen on this stuff. It's just a good place to have lunch. Well we always preferred the gardens, but what can you do with weather like this. What a summer!" She gestured scornfully at the procession of umbrellas and raincoats, trudging on across the wall opposite.

"It was after she saw the colour. She said it was just like that material Sally bought for her blouse. She seemed quite struck on that."

Anita had no interest in sewing talk. "She works here. I didn't know."

She knew Lou had cleaning jobs in offices round about but had never known she worked here at night. Yet obviously Cath and Mary did. Why was she always so out of things? Wasn't this her sanctuary? The one place in the world she belonged?

"Yes" Mary got out her knitting. "She cleaned the offices upstairs, but she did say she would pop down and have a look."

"Well. Was it playing at night?" Anita suddenly felt she needed to know if the umbrellas and raincoats did continue the journey while she was trying to sleep in her small bedsitting room – harassed by the noises of the house and the heartburn brought on by horrors at work. The thought would be oddly comforting.

After all, it was Art. You didn't turn Art off.

"I don't know. It was Tuesday week, we haven't seen her since then. She must have gone to her brother's early. You know, she said she was going down to Bognor to stay with him. Not that she was looking forward to it much. She can't get on with his wife you know, she's an impossible woman. But Bill is the only relative she has in the world. So she feels she must go sometimes. She would be all alone without him."

Anita remembered what Lou had said about those holidays, and felt that she was as alone with her brother as she was without him. But they were all lonely, that was the point. Even Cath, sparkling and abrasive in the group, was on her own in the world outside it.

"Yes, it was Sally who saw it change first." That was Cath, remembering. "It was the day Lou bought that lovely silk in to show us. She said she saw..."

"It wasn't just a colour though, I told you. She saw a face." Mary packed the last of her lunch boxes away before continuing. "She said just before one of the raincoats got to the end, the brolly tilted, and for a moment she saw the woman's face."

"Yes, that's right, and she said that suddenly the umbrella woman looked so happy, as if..." Cath let her sentence tail off wistfully. Perhaps she was having more than her fair share of trouble at work too?

"Really?" Anita was just being polite, she had no interest in the long ago Sally, just a kind of relief that she never turned up again. The others often spoke as if it was in some way Sally's room.

Would she have welcomed Anita as they had?

People usually did not. "Well, I hope it doesn't end, or they take it down, or whatever." She meant more than the Installation of course. She did not want these lunchtimes to end either.

8

They all looked gloomy at the thought of 'they', and packed their lunches slowly away. "See you all tomorrow then", said Anita hopefully.

"Yes." Cath, brisk as ever. "And I'll see you tonight Mary."

Noticing Anita's look, she said, rather defensively, "They are giving a talk on the art of weaving here tonight. We thought we would go. If we can, we'll sneak away and take a look in here for you and see if it's still running. Though I know it won't be."

That was said to humour her Anita knew. She was hurt that Cath had asked Mary to go with her. Yet surely anything to do with the art of the Gallery should have been for her not Mary, if they were to make these separate alliances. It unsettled her, but it did not surprise her.

She knew their lunch club would break up. It was only a matter of time. They would be sure to remove the Installation anyway. It wouldn't play on for ever. Someone would remember this little room, and that would be that.

Anita thought a lot about the Umbrella Room over her dull weekend. It rained incessantly. Her bed sit seemed smaller and noisier than ever. She dreaded the increasing inroads of the night as the days got shorter and shorter. And there was a dull kind of pain she didn't examine at the thought of Cath and Mary.

Did Cath find Mary better company than her? Even dull Mary?

It was just that it was a sewing thing she consoled herself, that's why she asked Mary, and tried to settle down and put herself to sleep with a book. But she couldn't lose herself in it tonight. She kept thinking about Cath's promise to pop in and see if the Installation was still playing.

She imagined Cath and Mary tiptoeing down the long

empty galleries. And thought how dark and empty they would be. They would creep through the small Mary sewing at a red checkered sandwich…Cath holding out something wonderful that vanished as Anita was pulled away by the tide of dawn – and yet again the weary trudge to the horrors of the office claimed her.

After a long and harrowing morning, the threatened redundancy hovering closer and closer, Anita escaped thankfully to the haven of the Gallery. She walked through the wet gardens, into the grand lobby, and handed over her dripping coat and brolly to the Cloakroom girl, as usual.

"Will this rain ever stop?" She usually forced herself to say something as she handed her coat over. The staff here weren't much on chatting, so it never got her involved in any conversations.

She walked through the galleries, emptier than usual, and rather cold today, through the arch at the back and along the corridor to the forgotten Installation Room. She took a deep breath before entering, the dread of finding it changed, or gone, strong upon her since the dreams of last night.

It was still playing. The ladies in the macs and brollies marched patiently across the wall into whatever lay beyond. But the room was empty. Cold and dark and empty. And so it stayed, through the long lunch hour.

Lou had not come back from her holidays. Well, she must have. But she had not come back here. Perhaps she had finally decided to go where she had family. Wouldn't I, if I could, thought Anita.

And Mary and Cath must have teamed up and gone off to a restaurant, just like normal people. Perhaps they were only here till they found that special lunchtime friend.

And so Anita found herself on her own again. Nothing ever seemed to last for her – so why had she felt that this would, that these quiet lunches would go on forever?

2 o clock came and went, but Anita sat on in the darkening Installation room, watching the hypnotic procession of umbrellas. She would not go back to work today. Something inside her was saying she would never go back to that office.

Why go back and get that looming redundancy notice in person. Let them post it to her. Let them post it to her here, if they wanted. She would sit silent, till the Gallery closed, thinking of nothing, soothed by the calm procession in front of her.

The wind howled round the building like a distant sea, and she could hear the rain hitting the windows of the big gallery. She felt safe and cocooned. No-one could fight their way through this to find her.

But there were no friends here for her now – only the surging umbrellas of the Installation. And even they seemed to be changing. Were they turning from neutral to unfriendly?

The two mackintoshed figures who had just appeared at the top left of the Installation and were starting their plod to the bottom right seemed a cruel reminder of Mary and Cath – arm in arm, like the team of two that had excluded her, they made their way across the wall ready to disappear with the rest.

Anita watched them process along, but right at the edge of the wall they seemed to hesitate and Anita thought she saw a movement of hand on umbrella, as if the taller figure was going to beckon her to come along with them.

Was she too going to see the Installation change, if only for a moment? She got up quickly and walked towards the wall. In all the weeks she had been coming, she had never got so close to it. Yes. Something was happening. And she, Anita, was the one to see it this time. There was no colour, just the monotonous grey and black, but the figures had not disappeared, they hesitated almost as if they were waiting for something.

By 5 o clock it was pitch dark outside, the wind hurtling round, and the staff busy bundling themselves into raincoats and umbrellas; longing for the warmth of home, but dreading the walk to the car park. Just before closing time, the wind blew a small lady done up like a waterproof bundle through the big gallery doors.

She didn't bother to shed her wet coat, just looked round, and, whistling softly to herself, walked up to Reception.

"Sally Piper" she was so quiet, it was almost a whisper, "my Installation… I've come to switch it off."

The woman looked at her blank, unseeing, and Sally floated softly past, through the galleries, through the small gloomy arch at the end and into the Installation Room.

The room was empty, apart from the raincoats that surged across the wall, umbrellas open, rain pelting down.

She reached up to the alcove where the player was, turning back before her hand reached the Open/Close button for one last look at the wall. And just for a moment, she caught sight of a pair of sad grey eyes under faded auburn hair, saw the face light up with joy, as the raincoated figure reached the end of the wall and hurried towards what lay beyond.

* * *

12

Author's note: *The Umbrellas of Hamelin* was a collaboration with the artist Bea Burchill, in that I wrote the story and it inspired her painting, the one which has been used as the book cover. We are presently working on a story about a canal boat, which will appear, moored up, apparently deserted in a great hurry. I am hoping it will inspire another Burchill painting.

Disraeli Crescent

It is Easter Monday in Disraeli Crescent, though not necessarily that day anywhere else, and Miss Prudence Wilmot is getting ready to go to early morning Service.

In the potting shed down the garden next door, Geoffrey Gormless is sitting hunched over the old workbench he uses for his writing desk. Uneaten bluebottles mummify in spiders' webs over his head. His pen moves rapidly over the paper. He must write while he can, for soon Mrs. Gormless will be woken by her imminent and fateful alarm clock and his freedom will be over.

"Master, I beg you, just one more time" pleads voluptuous blonde Desiree, her heaving bosom surging through the torn bodice of her designer frock. Geoff the CEO smiles suavely, he has taken his fill of her and…

"GEOFFREY, GEOFFREY GORMLESS!"

"Coming, pet, at once."

Readjusting his glasses, Geoff the Barbarian sets off up the garden path at a brisk trot. He will catch hell from Mrs. G. if he is late for his bacon and eggs.

In his rented room upstairs Aziz Khan is getting up. Gloomily. His personal morning preference would be to sleep in until June and what the English laughably call Summer, but the terrifying and loud alarm clock of his terrifying and loud landlady forbids it.

In a corner of the dusty potting shed a Venusian spins idly at its web. The moonlings will blunder into its netting and it will catch them. Although it has no use for them at all.

14

You can't take over a planet without making webs.

Celia next door – Celia of the weekly newspaper column – is also bored as she sits in her rapidly cooling bath. Today is the deadline for the famous column and so far the week's amusing domestic incident has simply failed to occur. She has nothing at all to write about. Being got out of the bath at an inconveniently early hour and then locking herself out clad in a scanty towel is beginning to look like her only option.

As Miss Prudence Wilmot struggles to close the huge front door behind her, she considers the Crescent in which she lives.

It seems to her that she used to know everyone; that each stone house used to contain a family, and the pavement used to blaze with hopscotch squares.

Was it like that once? Or will it be like that someday? And how did I get stranded here, she wonders. This is a Crescent built for families, not for ladies of a certain age, who live on their own. Who have no husband, no children and no career. By no stretch of the imagination can her routine office job be called a career.

Walking down the path she notices the postman toiling up Celia's drive with an enormous parcel. Whatever can it be, she wonders, but doesn't connect it with the latest amusing domestic mishap. She assumes that by now the column will have been written. If she realises the dramatic scene that is about to be enacted, she will surely stay and watch, and be late for the Service.

"DO YOU CALL THOSE HANDS CLEAN!"

Mrs. G's enormous voice shatters the holiday calm.

Geoff the CEO stares at the stained glass of the bathroom window as he dries his hands.

Voluptuous blonde Desiree is bringing him breakfast; his designer coffee. Raw. She places it in front of him and tremblingly waits to see if it will please him. With a lift of his groomed eyebrow, Geoff the CEO tiptoes downstairs so as not to annoy Mrs. G. and eats up his overcooked egg and underdone bacon.

At one end of Disraeli Crescent is the church with its vicarage. At the other end is a shopping precinct. There is even a restaurant where you can get a rather bad Italian meal and morning coffee. The Benjamino.

Lunchtime in Disraeli Crescent sees Miss Prudence Wilmot opening a tin of baked beans. Somehow, she thinks, this doesn't seem suitable for Easter Monday. Surely she should be boiling a chicken to be set before an appreciative curate?

Geoffrey Gormless is sitting unhappily in the aforementioned restaurant while Mrs. G. chomps through a cartwheel of doughy pastry covered with sticky cheese. For once Desiree is not with him. He is dreaming wistfully of the days when he and Mrs G. used to sit down to a roast dinner. And pizzas and health food and batter fried chicken had never been invented.

Tick tock goes the spider in the restaurant clock.

Beep Beep Beep Meep Meep Meep, goes Aziz Khan's electronic watch. He looks at it anxiously. It has got completely out of control and is about to do something appalling like speaking his weight or playing Space Invaders with itself.

Oh where is the Barbara Woodhouse of the Electronic Watch World, he sighs. He could take it to her Obedience

Classes. She would give one firm jerk at its strap and it would go back to simply telling the time. He has never been able to find out what the time is since the fateful day he got the watch.

Though he feels that it is bound to be too late.

Sadly, he resumes his biscuit lunch.

The Venusian is lying back in its web, its eight little jackbooted feet up, contemplating the struggles of a moonling that has blundered into its camouflage netting. It will have no lunch and need no lunch.

Celia is dreaming of a wine bar somewhere in Islington.

Darlings! I NEVER thought I'd get back into the house!!! You should have SEEN the look on the postman's face. I swear my TITS were falling out at one extreme, and at the other extreme…

But her voice tails off – discouraged. The man of the moment will not look at her. Not even in her daydreams. He is watching the young girls come and go; looking at his watch discreetly, but not discreetly enough.

Sometimes she feels that her public too are beginning to look at their watches, and then what will become of her?

She goes to phone her copy in anyway. There is nothing else she can do.

In his Vicarage, the Vicar lies dead, slumped over the desk in his library. Choked; strangled. His face black, his swollen tongue protruding. The broken grandfather clock stares at the scene, the only witness. The au pair, who has just discovered the body, puts the tray down, leans over and tears at the sticky webbing that covers his throat.

Miss Prudence Wilmot puts her library book down with a sigh. She had hoped for something in the Agatha Christie style. The vicar dead in his study, yes. But nothing too graphic in the way of details. This book will take her all the way through the post mortem; the smell of blood and rotting food from dead gut will permeate the pages. And there is a strong suggestion of science fiction too. Which is a genre she dislikes very much.

Perhaps the only way to obtain the books you want to read is to write them yourself, she thinks.

Soon it will be bedtime in Disraeli Crescent.

Lights have been coming on in various rooms, suppers are being prepared.

"GEOFFREY, HAVE YOU FINISHED THAT HOOVERING?"

"Yes, pet."

"WELL. I HOPE ITS DONE PROPERLY."

Mrs. G. looms over him.

Geoffrey Gormless thinks that the most erotic thing in the world would be to be with a woman who is smaller than him. She wouldn't have to have a voluptuous bosom or a torn designer bodice. She wouldn't have to tremble in his presence. Just looking pleased to see him would do.

"AND STOP YOUR DAYDREAMING. I WANT EVERYTHING RIGHT BEFORE WE GO TO BED. I'VE NEVER KNOWN ANYTHING LIKE IT FOR SPIDERS WEBS. ALL OVER THE PLACE. ALL THE YEAR ROUND. IF WE'D TAKEN THAT FLAT NEXT DOOR TO MY MOTHER, LIKE I WANTED, WE…"

Geoffrey Gormless looks more and more depressed. It's his birthday today, and he can see he isn't going to get his present if she gets set on this tack.

He decides to throw the lodger to the lion. His birthday comes but once a year he excuses himself.

"I think Mr. Khan has been eating biscuits in his room again, pet. I found the vacuum quite choked with crumbs."

Mrs. G. roars off, distracted from her reproaches about the neat little flat they should have bought. It is possible that Geoff the Barbarian should have listened to her at the time.

Are mothers in law more dangerous than Venusians?

Miss Prudence Wilmot in her sensible candlewick dressing gown and matching slippers, is making herself the bedtime cup of cocoa, without which she finds it impossible to sleep.

She wishes in a vague sort of way that she were more like Celia next door, whose aids to sleep are so much more sophisticated. She always takes sleeping pills and simple CAN'T get off without them DARLINGS.

"…or a really satisfactory …"

Celia stops bothering. Even her imaginary lovers now doze and snore, instead of falling passionately upon her. She will get up and pace the bedroom all night, wondering whether she should gives the guy in Sales some encouragement after all.

Bit of a comedown though. Surely she, Celia, can do better than that? At any rate she needs another pill. What a DREARY day it's been. What a DREARY day it always is!

Perched precariously on top of Mrs. G., Geoffrey Gormless is celebrating his birthday.

Voluptuous blonde Desiree will have to sleep alone tonight, unwarmed by the arms of her suave master.

Mrs. G. cries out, her voice filled with real passion.

"GEOFFREY GORMLESS, YOU'VE MADE A DREADFUL JOB OF PAINTING THAT CEILING!!"

Mummified bluebottles hang in webs. Venusians are awake.

Aziz Khan groans in his sleep. He is dreaming that he is a biscuit crumb and Mrs G. is a hoover. His watch is quenched in a glass of water beside his bed.

He knows the danger of unguarded watches.

Geoff the CEO is feeling chilly in the early hours of the morning. The enormous form of Mrs G. is hogging the kingsize duvet. It is an exceptionally cold April. He makes a half-hearted attempt to pull some back. She is a devil when roused out of a deep sleep.

Tick tock, tick tock, tick tock, the spider climbs up the clock.

The small hours come to Disraeli Crescent.

Desiree slips out into the cold of the primeval dawn to fetch firewood so that she will have Geoff the CEO's fashionable coffee hot and ready the instant he awakes from his designer sleep.

Aziz Khan's dreams get worse and worse. Too late, too late, too late, his watch splutters in the water. It has tried and tried to warn him.

Brrrr Brrrr The discreet and apologetic sound of Miss Prudence Wilmot's alarm clock wakes her up.

She gets up conscientiously. There is a church service to attend.

It is Easter Monday in Disraeli Crescent. Though not necessarily that day anywhere else.

* * *

The Martian Goes to a Party and has a Nice Day

"And what's your wife's name, Ray?" asked blonde Sandra. Kindly.

Not Ray, thought the Martian from its usual sidelines position, but Ravi. Surely. But of course, it is a little difficult for them to say.

Sandra repeated the answer disbelievingly.

"San Tie… er… Shanni," with a ripple of bemused laughter.

Did they learn this kind of thing at school? The Martian experimented quietly to itself. No, it couldn't manage even one mispronunciation of a name as simple as Shantih, let alone two.

"Bet you're glad you asked that, Sandra." Her husband, beamed, avuncular, from the sidelines. "She'll never learn. She asked how to spell Tad's name the other day. All those consonants!"

The party was getting under way.

As the Martian murmured its hellos and grabbed a glass of something, it wished there was a button it could press marked REPLAY.

It could wind the conversation back to the moment where blonde Sandra said: "And what's your wife's name, Ray?"

Then it would press DELETE and INSERT and have Ravi answer, "Ann."

The object of the exercise would be to see how far they would get with the "How do you spell THAT?" and "I'll bet you're glad you asked that!" routine before they realised what had actually been said.

Could they manage the two creative mispronunciations of "Ann" that were essential to the ritual?

The U.S. contingent was still separate, clustered under the banner that said:

BOYS WE ARE PLEASED AND PROUD TO HAVE YOU WITH US TONITE!

They were entertaining the U.S.Navy, and the British contingent had been overruled on their choice of banner, which would have read,

HELLO SAILOR

Americans were completely outclassed in these introductory put downs anyway. A double mispronunciation of Shantih just after you have introduced yourself as Hackenbacker J. Marlinspiker the Third was too difficult for the human brain to encompass. Or so the Martian had deduced.

It wandered into the kitchen to say hello to Tiswas, a furry earthling of whom it was very fond, but the kitchen was full of Sharran Ellen, hot-faced, pushing and pulling pot luck contributions in and out of ovens.

Upon offering to help, the Martian was put to work carrying the dead pig that was de rigeur at expat parties.

"Now folks, we are all going to get acquainted as quickly as possible. We're going to play a party game."

No mingling was taking place at all, but Sharran Ellen had everything in hand.

The Martian, in its panic to get back to the safety of the kitchen, missed the rest. But, after chopping at a little more pig, it decided that, in the interests of its scientific research, it must steel itself to at least observe.

Sharran Ellen had excelled herself. They were all having

the names of different countries pinned on them. Martian research would go well tonight. It wandered cautiously round the room, reading people's backs. It hoped no-one had thought to add the Planet Mars, which did not get a very good press.

Ah yes, there was the host country. The country that had employed them all at large salaries and in luxury accommodation, thus giving grave earthling offense. It would come in for a lot of stick tonight.

A quick trip back to the deserted kitchen enabled the Martian to remove the label from its own back. As there was no such country as Rhodesia, it felt justified in throwing the label into the waste-bin.

Now, safely anonymous again, it could wander about and discover who was really for it tonight.

Puzzlingly, it seemed to be the Mexicans.

What could they have done to deserve all the abuse that was heaped upon them?

The Martian was enlightened by an even hotter and louder Sharran Ellen.

They were Spanish speakers. They spoke Spanish.

The Martian was pleased to note that its deduction that Mexicans were just the representatives for the peoples of Central America (and presumably Spain) in general was correct, but alarmed to find that Spanish speaking was a crime.

That was what made it so nervous. It could never predict what would be a crime next. What would happen if it suddenly started to speak in its long-forgotten native tongue? Would that be OK, or not? They always seemed to know, but how did they find out?

Discreetly (it hoped) the Martian moved nearer to catch the details of the accusation.

"Why, they should become Americans. All of us who came, we became Americans. We didn't just stay as we were,"

The Martian began to understand the crime of the Spanish speakers.

When the first immigrants to the Americas had come, they had had the decency to become Americans. They had learnt the language of the Sioux, the Cheyenne, the Mohican; they had learnt to hunt the buffalo with bow and arrow. They had lived in tepees and learnt the rain dances. They had left their European ways behind them. But now these Spanish speaking people were refusing to do this.

They would not learn to speak the language of the Sioux, the Cheyenne, the Mohican. They refused the rain dance, the tepee, the bow and arrow. They seemed to want to bring their own ways and their own language with them.

Some tentative mingling was taking place now, because the Brits had had much the same problem. In the last centuries, they had gone to Africa, to Asia, to India, where they too had conformed to the customs of the lands in which they found themselves.

They had spoken Swahili, Urdu, worn the sari. Indeed, they had worn nothing at all but leaves where that had seemed culturally appropriate. And now, to their horror, all these ungrateful people were coming – no they were flooding – flooding was definitely the consensus word – flooding in, and refusing to conform to the culture of the Brits.

Probably they were all Spanish speakers too.

As a completely illegal immigrant itself, the Martian felt strangely unqualified to join in the Spanish speaker conversation. Could one Martian qualify as a flood? It had never yet come across another.

Sighing, it gave up on the socialising and decided to do what it always did at parties.

It would go outside and look for its spaceship.

It knew that the ship would come one day. On that Nice Day that it was always being ordered to have.

Outside it was quiet. And cool. Wandering down the garden path upon which armies of tiny Venusians struggled with their new wings, it was joined by Tiswas, that furry, four-legged, un-fallen Earth person, who the Martian truly loved.

Together they watched the Venusians struggle with their wings. There were so many of them that Tiswas had long ago lost interest in pouncing on them. Even in their difficulties, the Venusians did not look clumsy or weak. They kept their air of contained and icy invulnerability at all times.

They were sure they had already won the battle for the planet.

They were certainly winning the propaganda battle. The earthlings now equated Mars with war, and Venus with love.

Watching the great wheels of palm sway against the beautiful sky, a sky more full of bright stars than any it could remember seeing, the Martian wondered about the skies of Mars, feeling vaguely hopeful. A winter party night, when everyone was so busy indoors, would be ideal.

No-one would see the ship land or take off again with the Martian and Tiswas safely aboard.

Not that it would matter really if anyone did see. They all drank so much here that a space ship would go into the same category as a pink elephant.

Sharran Ellen's voice filled the night silence.

"We're here to civilise these people!"

She was drunk now, and shouting.

Looking down into the moonlit desert behind the house, the Martian thought of all the people who lived there. Nomadic peoples, in their tents. Uncivilized people who hadn't yet got coca cola, graffiti, football hooliganism, the Ku Klux Klan, snuff movies, child pornography…"

Deprived people?

For good or ill, Western civilisation was coming closer now, its breath hot and eager, its foot firmly in the door, its carpetbag full of glossy treasures enticingly open. Depraved people? But it would not bring paradise. So where then was paradise? Not here, not there. Not in the East nor in the West – maybe it was only to be found on the warm red sands of Mars.

But a sudden flash of lightning lit up the strange sky, sending Tiswas scurrying, fur all abristle, anxious they should get back inside the kitchen before the rain started.

They ran down the path, scattering the Venusians, who, the Martian was alarmed to see, had formed themselves into little letters saying: "MARTIAN GO HOME", and "DIE, MARTIAN SCUM".

Thunder followed so quickly on the lightning flash that they were only just inside the kitchen when great raindrops began to batter furiously at the windows, silencing the party for a few seconds.

Shutting the door on the storm, the Martian thought about the vast sky, and the voice that had spoken from it.

"No ship tonight, Tiswas. But not to worry, it will come. One day."

"Do you want to come with me to Mars, Tiswas?"

"AsGodWills" purred Tiswas agreeably, as he made for his bowl.

* * *

Author's note: I hesitated over including this story, which reflects my shock at my first experience of expat life, nearly thirty five years ago. I have changed a lot since then, and would write about it very differently now. Also us expats are such easy targets. But I wanted to keep it in as it is also an expression of feeling a stranger in a strange land, even among my fellow countrymen in expat exile. It was one of the things that made me start to wonder about myself. Also it contains our fierce and lovely cat Whites, featuring as Tiswas, who gets the last word. The problem is not my fellow expats, but me. And I came to be very fond of very many of them.

Talky Tin

Talky Tin sat in the window seat looking inscrutable.

At least that's how everyone said he looked. And then they said what mysterious creatures cats are.

But, although she had tried very hard to see what was inscrutable about him, Emily hadn't been able to so far.

To her, he seemed very easy to read.

When he was happy he purred and smiled. When he was hungry, he wailed and bellowed.

When he was sleepy, he fell asleep. He fell asleep on the instant, wherever he was. Emily had found him slumped by his food bowl; upside down in the flower bed; snoring happily under the feeder while the birds pecked around him.

He loved people, climbing and purring over all visitors. Falling asleep on them if he was sleepy. Wailing at them if he was hungry.

Apparently, to be true to his inscrutable type, he should only have sat on those visitors who were allergic to cats. But everyone was an acceptable cat couch to Talky.

He detested all cats.

And he was not at all inscrutable about making that known. He didn't even bother to go through the elaborate fight rituals of his kind. He fired no warning shots across the bows. Any cat coming within the invisible line Talky had drawn around the property met a business like set of claws and teeth instantly.

They left quickly. And didn't come back.

All in all, Emily thought that Talky was probably from another planet. And he hadn't bothered to do his homework properly. Or perhaps he was just very lazy about his camouflage.

Yet no-one had noticed.

No-one, apart from her. And apparently she didn't matter.

Which left a nagging worry in her mind. If Talky knew that she didn't matter, did that mean that he had spotted her?

* * *

Publisher's note: *Talky Tin* was first published by Fantastic Books Publishing in the flash fiction anthology, Kaleidoscope.

The Rainy Day House

"It rained and rained and rained
The average fall was well maintained
And when the tracks were simply bogs
It started raining cats and dogs
After a drought of half an hour
We had a most refreshing shower
And then most curious thing of all
A gentle rain began to fall
Next day but one was fairly dry
Save for one deluge from the sky
Which wetted the party to the skin
And then at last the rain set in."

Alan had pinned the verse, by that prolific poet Anon, to the dashboard, and the words went maddeningly round and round in Marta's head, to a counterpoint of squeaking wipers that were failing to keep the windscreen clear.

She needed to think. About many things. And she didn't want to talk. She had said all she needed to say to Alan about this trip.

It was odd, his buying that poem. It only seemed a step up from buying notices saying "You Don't Have To Be Mad To Work Here, But It Helps". There had been quite a vogue for those when she started her working life.

You could be sure then that in the most drab of conventional offices, they would have at least one of the You

Don't Have To Be Mad notices installed. And the notice was a reliable warning that, when someone in the office did something truly exceptional, like put sweeteners in their coffee or forgot where they left the stapler, there would be a chorus of "We're all mad here."

Was it sixteen years ago?

The years stood like stones between then and now. The Marta of those days was gone as surely as.... as surely as this rain... wasn't.

And now Alan was slowing down. At last. The rain was already washing away the sides of the road. Streams of leaves and small pebbles had appeared, followed by larger stones, that were soon, Marta was sure, to be followed by boulders, then the road would be blocked.

And this coast was deserted. Well, she had said it all to Alan. They would have to turn back, return to the cold, comfortless little guest house and just see how quickly they could drive out of here. Although the airport was a few days drive away. Worryingly.

She simply couldn't wait to get back. Everything was waiting for her there.

They came to a stop and Alan began to drive into a gap in the trees. "I think you'd be better backing up Alan. Do you want me to get out?" It came out rather cold and clipped. But why shouldn't it?

He looked at her, almost with eagerness. "No. I'm turning off for the glacier. Didn't you see the sign?"

How could I see anything in this, Marta thought. And I just don't believe Alan, that you are actually going to try and get to this glacier! Why? Up this little track? With the rain pouring down in torrents? When the road itself is almost impassable?

What came out of her mouth was icy enough to put the glacier to shame. "You aren't turning back then. We are going to see this glacier."

They were statements. Not questions. And, wisely, Alan didn't respond, but concentrated on trying to see where he was going.

I loved this boyish eagerness once, thought Marta. I adored it.

Alan, so big and tall and blond. So broad in the shoulder. She still loved to look at him, and his mellow, adult profile. And these boyish enthusiasms had only seemed to enhance the man.

They still did. But only in their place. And this was neither the time nor the place.

Why holiday here for a start? And so early in Spring? It was freezing. There was snow on the high passes with more to come. She supposed she had to be glad this was rain falling and not snow. But it might prove as damaging in the long run.

The car juddered, and jolted and shuddered up the track. It was still early morning, and very dark in the forest.

Marta peered ahead between the frantic wipers. "Alan, we'd have to ford this bit. We'll have to turn back."

.The flood ahead was almost a relief.

"No, we'll be OK Marta. She's a four wheel drive remember. She can go anywhere."

Alan whooped childishly, and gunned the car towards the flood.

Which turned out to be much shallower than it looked. But the car stopped anyway.

As the engine died away and refused to come back to life, Marta felt a certain triumph through her panic. She had told him so. She had also told him that the mobile would not work out here, and when that was established to Alan's satisfaction, he returned sodden from another trip behind the bonnet to find Marta staring grimly at the petrol gauge.

"I blame myself, Alan" Marta said, in a level voice. "I should have checked last night. That little gas station was open late. We had no chance of filling up this morning, as we left so early. And, I had noticed that there is nothing else on this coast anyway."

All things that you should have done Alan. And failed to do.

Marta shivered as she watched Alan's back disappear into the torrent. The jerry can swung in his hands, rain drumbeating on it. He looked like he had swum a length or two by the time he disappeared into the trees.

I shouldn't have said those things. He has such a lot on his mind now. My next career move is so hard on him. But so good for me. And us. It will be good for us. I wouldn't consider it otherwise. Really I wouldn't.

How easy it was to say this in Alan's absence.

In the absence of anyone. And it might be morning, but the woods are as dark as midnight.

The sound of the rain was hypnotic. Call this Spring. Winter was waiting in there to pounce again. She drew the wonderfully soft sheepskin rug tighter round her. Thank goodness they had had time to do some shopping on the island.

They had stopped at a curious little place – an old Station waiting room – filled with beautiful leathers and wools. And jumpers displayed like art in a gallery. Alan would be thankful for that leather jacket she had talked him into buying…

The leathers had glowed out of the dark room – the sky had been heavy with rain even then. It reminded her for a happy moment of Bangkok silks, shining in that steamy heat.

The thought came to Marta that, if only it was warm, she could happily go to sleep, and sleep all day, if necessary.

And that's a terrible thought. Don't tell me middle age is setting in already. When I have I ever slept during the day? I am Marta, the Dynamo, I can keep going on 5 hours sleep. I can sell all day and party all night. Poor Alan just can't keep up.

You're just like your mother Marta, he would say. Which made her laugh, as she was nothing like her mother. Not even physically. Carmel was like mum. Pretty, blonde, … hopeless.

She was like her tall, dark, dashing father. Who certainly dashed away quickly enough, once he could. And can I blame him. That house. Full of Carmel and the girls. And the baby, crying all the time.

And her mother's endless, obsessive cleaning. That never stopped, night or day, as the years went on.

Marta and Alan had tiptoed back one time to find her setting things right for the morning in the spotless strait-jacketed kitchen.

She hadn't even seemed to register that is was 2 a.m. Much to their relief. And the baby wasn't crying for once.

Only it was. It seemed to be screaming now. Howling even. And I will have to get up and see to her, as no-one else will.

Marta jerked awake, her arm striking against the wheel. An arm clad in light maroon wool, for a moment melding into her schoolgirl dressing gown. The wind crying round the car.

I was asleep. Dreaming. She hadn't realised how tired she was.

It wasn't like Alan to have left her here. Although, what else to do? Given the foolish situation he had got them into. Dangerous and foolish. To run out of petrol, in territory like this. The little track – what she could make out of it through the torrents of rainwater – was turning into a stream.

These woods were amazing. The vegetation was more curly than back home – Sort of layered, and wheeled, with a strange tone to the green.

Have I ever been so alone in my life before? She thought of Alan's shoulders set angrily in his sodden jacket as he disappeared into the wet. And what they had said to each other.

Mile upon mile upon mile of virgin rain forest; mile upon mile upon mile of white sandy beaches. Cold grey sea lashing at cold white shore. They hadn't even passed a car. Not a gas station. It was going to take Alan hours to get back.

Alan wouldn't be pleased by "gas station". She could hear him saying "We are not in Manhattan yet, Mizz Marta."

Didn't you start to hallucinate if you were on your own too long?

Well, she had better keep rational about this. One of them going through a temporary madness was bad enough. She was perfectly safe here for a while. Even this rain would stop sometime. This was a track, not a stream bed; so whatever it looked like, she would not be washed away. There wasn't a soul around. And if there had been, they would simply be hikers. Not multiple murderers, or serial rapists.

They might bore me to death, but that would be it.

The sound of her giggling out loud jarred her.

Keep calm. Be rational.

If only this rain would stop and I could SEE something.

As if on cue, a massive gust of wind seemed to sweep aside

the clouds for a moment. The rain lightened, the trees stilled, making room for weak daylight to enter the rainforest.

And Marta did see something. Through the curly dripping trees. A glimpse of light?

Then sky darkened – and the rain returned, doubling its force. It's like monsoon. Do they have spring monsoon here? At least in the East, its warm, it's refreshing. This is like England tripled.

I did see a light didn't I? Almost like a restaurant or motel or something just up ahead?

No – surely, it's a rainforest mirage? If there are such things. What would a rainforest mirage be? Not an oasis. Obviously not green trees and running water! A wardrobe full of dry clothes perhaps and a hot bath.

Marta laughed out loud again and suddenly felt better.

I did see a light. A lighted window? Something? A building anyway, with someone in it. And a phone?

The next gust caught the car and rocked it. It was like going through a car wash. Bucket and buckets of water ran down the windows.

The next pause and I'm going to have a look, Marta thought. If there is anything there, anything, I'm going inside, I'm using their phone and getting some kind of vehicle out here. I don't care what it costs. Then I'll head back for the guest house and pick up Alan on the way.

I should never have left it to him. He just went rushing back down the track, when it would have been better to head for the glacier itself. After all, it is a tourist attraction in its way – there has to be something up there.

The weather wasn't being co-operative though. Amazingly, the force of the rain re-doubled and the sky grew even darker.

Well, at least this trip is giving me plenty of time to think. Which is what you want, isn't it Marta, she told herself.

Rationality. Think things through. That was Marta's watchword. She would never leap before she looked. Unlike most people in the world, it seemed to her.

But her body had leapt ahead of her. Without planning, without thought. She had been sick for the last five mornings. Sick and bloated.

She was pregnant. She didn't need tests and kits and doctors. She knew. She was pregnant.

She even knew exactly when it happened. Alan would be thrilled when she told him. If she told him.

Marta knew her panic had an irrational element.

She had watched both her mother and her elder sister struggle. With small children, and no reliable help.

Three little girls Carmel had had. When Matt had left her. Tessa, four, and Isabelle and Anneliese the twins, three.

She had had to come home. Marta could remember her mother's horror even now.

Marta had watched her beautiful, elder sister trying to cope with the little girls. In the three-bedroom semi-detached that was always kept as neat as an advert.

And then she had heard her throwing up in the bathroom, morning after morning.

Its always girls in our family if you have morning sickness, her gran had said grimly. Always.

Apparently, if Heidi had been a son, Matt might have returned to resume his responsibilities.

Fat chance of that, thought the Marta of now and of then.

Never, never, never. Never will this happen to me, she had thought.

And now, against every plan and expectation she was pregnant. They hadn't intended this to happen for a couple of years yet. Not with the Manhattan project just starting up. That could lead her to heights undreamed of, even in the triumphs of her city days. And whatever could be said for London, New York is where it all is. There is simply no contest. We have to go. And I can't be pregnant.

But I'm not on my own. I'm not 24. I'm not widowed or abandoned. I'm 36, and can't leave it too much longer before we have our child. We have money – we will soon be rich. I'm not married to Matt. I'm married to Alan. A good man. A caring man. Ian. This ridiculous holiday – a last fling before Manhattan! – is out of character.

Up to now they had spent their holidays on the beach somewhere. Baking. Truly relaxing. Or else they had had the sort of holiday that made everyone else gasp. Their Icelandic trek for instance. Although sadly that seemed to have fuelled Alan's glacial obsession, instead of quenching it.

But this pregnancy. It couldn't have come at a worse time. And Alan would snatch at any chance, any opportunity,… face facts Marta.

He doesn't want us to go. He doesn't want to sell the business and move to New York.

A great gust of wind almost flattened the mass of trees in front of her and swept the windscreen clear for a moment.

And, there, through the trees, was the light. Definitely and clearly a light. Someone lived there.

A house. Out here!

No. It must be a kind of guest house, or restaurant. The Glacier Centre. Undoubtedly.

GLACIER WORLD perhaps, with people in penguin

costumes doing pageants on the hour. And A GLACIER EXPERIENCE that made it quite unnecessary to see the real thing.

Marta laughed at herself. I must admit to feeling full of cheerfulness and well-being since all this started. In spite of the sickness. And this sudden tiredness

What a relief. Because whatever that is, its for tourists, and its open. Next lull and I'm going to run for it.

Marta pulled up the collar of her light waterproof jacket; pulled the rug over her head and waited.

The wind cracked like thunder and blew the rain clear away for a moment. The light was free to pull at Marta. It had an odd, pretty, stained glass glow. Or was it just an effect of the rain?

She sprang from the car, splashed through water on pebbles, waded past trees splashing her, the wind pulling her back, the rain returning. It was almost like swimming. Please be open, please be open.

Just please let someone be at home.

It was further away than it looked. Marta almost felt panic. It was impossible to see now if there was light. The thought of taking a wrong turning in this pathless forest....

Please God that Alan would have the sense to keep to the road.

If I just keep going up this track; up this stream, soon to be a river, I will find the light. If it was a light. And more importantly, I will know exactly how to get back to the car.

She daren't look back because she knew she would see nothing but glimpses of dark curly trees through torrents of water.

Marta stopped, gasping for breath. It was like trying to

breathe underwater. There was nowhere to shelter now. The rainforest canopy was just a gigantic sieve, apparently channeling everything that fell onto Marta's head.

The path, stream, whatever it was, was getting steeper now. Everything on the Island seemed to be on the side of a mountain. It was hard going. Hard even to keep balanced.

Marta slipped on wet stones, and found herself hanging desperately on to a wooden balustrade. There were wooden steps in front of her, then a wooden balcony, and double glass doors, like a waterfall.

And a sign. Glowing out of rain.

THE RAINY DAY HOUSE.

Marta pushed at the doors. And, Thank God, Thank God, they yielded. And she was through into a dry world. A scrubbed pine hall – clean and warm.

She stood carefully on the matting, looking round.

The pine was warm and gold. Marta wanted to warm her hands at the racks of harlequin ski suits and orange climbing gear.

Postcards glowed on their stands. Lovely postcards, she thought approvingly. Foxgloves with the mountain behind – so perfectly saturated with light. Mount Cook at sunrise. She had already sent several of those.

"You've been out in the wet alright." The cheerful Oz voice was warming too.

Odd. The Rainy Day House seemed almost to grow out of the forest. But its proprietor was a transplant, not an islander at all.

"You'll be wet right through. Get a coffee inside you, and then you can have a bath and get some dry clothes on."

Proprietor: Mrs Maura McNeale announced the sign at

Reception. And the lady at the desk matched the name. Her hair must have been bright red once; and her fair freckled face had seen too much sun.

Hers was a complexion most suited to rain forest climes. Marta was grateful for her pale olive skin and dark eyes. She could soak up the sun. Soak it up as these trees soaked up the deluges that fell on them.

Oh, but the smell of coffee. Good coffee. That seemed as warming as anything. There was a restaurant in one corner. Its neat little pine chairs and table all clean and scrubbed; its cushions and cloths brightly checked and sprigged. Marta could smell freshly baked croissants too. Out here!

Maura McNeale bustled ahead of her, clearing some cups and plates off one of the round honey coloured tables. So, even as early as this they had visitors. In this weather.

But it was The Rainy Day House after all.

Marta felt sharply hungry all of a sudden, her sickness gone. Now what could that mean? Was this morning sickness or wasn't it. She tried to tell herself it wasn't important. And what Gran had said all those years ago was just ridiculous. But... if it's a girl. A son would fit so much better with her... their plans. And there was only time for one child.

Well, now, Marta. You can stop putting all this off. And think things through. You actually have time. All day, I wouldn't be surprised. And you can think over a hot breakfast. It was a holiday after all.

She shook as much water off as she could and settled in a corner of the restaurant that was fragrant with the smell of good coffee. And pine. And polish.

I feel at home here. For the first time since we arrived on this coast. There is something Tyrolean about this place.

Although there is nothing ostensibly Tyrolean about the freckled Mrs McNeale.

She set coffee and croissants, butter and jam in front of Marta. "I've put you out some towels and a dressing gown in the pink bathroom, and you can put your wet clothes in the machine there."

This was Tyrolean organization alright. Mrs. Maura McNeale really ought to have golden plaits wound round her head and a dirndl, instead of her sensible blue jeans. Marta resolved to ask her about herself when she had got dry again.

Everything is so clean, so well-organised. Marta approved the long pine staircase, with its wide treads, solid balustrade; and the wide landing, with its bedrooms and bathrooms, all colour-coded.

"Here's the laundry room. Your stuff'll be done and dry in no time."

Mrs. McNeale bustled off, leaving Marta in a pine-scented silence, broken only the purring hum of a washing machine.

This household wakes up early. Marta approved of that. Time was so precious. Never waste a minute.

But still it was good to have time to stop and think. Guilt-free time. For what else could I be doing? Marta asked the pale pink ceiling. She felt a little guilty for soaking in the hot bath. She was very much a power shower person as a rule.

Hard to think in a shower though.

David Alan. David Alan. The name echoed softly across the pink tiles. It did sound right. A son would fit so well.

Girls were something of a wild card. David Alan could go to his father's old school to start with – Alan would be very happy with that. And she thought he could accept her further plans for American education.

42

Their son would have the best of both worlds. That was important. He would be an American, but with an English edge to him.

But if they had a girl…. Alan would never agree to a daughter going away to school for a start. And how was she, Marta, to manage? This project was going to consume all her energies for quite some time.

The problems all her friends were having with in-house child-minders! And apparently it was even more difficult in NY.

What a relaxing bath this was. And such a sleepy, soft pink room.

All the accoutrements to Marta's bath were personalized. A soft honeyed cream, with The Rainy Day House picked out in plain gold lettering. The large fluffy towels were cream, with tiny gold initials in the corners.

Yes. These would go happily in all the different bathrooms.

The bath foam had a subtle scent of Spring. Both invigorating and relaxing.

And what a view. She was high up, looking out over the top of the forest, full into the Southland skies. The skies of late Spring, clouds racing towards Summer, against the deep clear blue.

What colour was London? It was grey. Just grey. All its tinsel couldn't hide its greyness. But New York was warm browns. Perhaps she and Alan should look further – try to find something in one of those lovely brownstone buildings.

The salary she had been promised made it ridiculous for Alan to worry about selling the bookshop. He would have every chance in NY. And, anyway, he wouldn't need to earn anything, if he didn't want to.

He could browse through his old books; almost play at being a book dealer.

How would she decorate their flat? It would have a wonderful sweep of space, looking out over the tall city. It would take some thinking about, some care. Warm silks, glowing out of dark wood. NY was as warm and humid as the tropics sometimes. And sometimes as cold as … Rainforest.

Marta suddenly realized where she was. This water is cold too. Have I been asleep? She groped for her watch, remembering she had left it in the car. Her expensive tiny gold watch!

Not that there is a soul around to steal it. So stop worrying Marta, and start thinking about what you ought to be thinking about.

The word lunch came unbidden into her mind. I'm hungry. Me. Marta. I don't eat. I just nibble occasionally as I fly past. And now all I can think about is food. And sleep.

The scent of Spring coaxed Marta back down to the lobby. There were freesias banked everywhere downstairs.

"Always makes me think of Perth in the Spring. They used to grow in drifts out in the bush there."

"How lovely" Marta's homes were never without fresh flowers, beautifully arranged. "You miss Perth then Mrs. McNeale.?"

"Oh, call me Maura. Everyone does. Yes, I do. Sometimes. Lived in Perth all my life. We came here, the girls and me, after my husband died. It seemed a way to make a living. Matt was a good man, but he didn't leave us much beyond the house."

Another Matt who left his wife and children unsupported! But admit, Marta, that that will never be your situation.

Alan has taken care of that, as he takes care of everything. I shouldn't have said that about the petrol. I really shouldn't.

"Will you have lunch, I've just freshened up the buffet."

Mrs McNeale's words startled Marta. "I must have fallen asleep in that bath. I had no idea it was lunch time."

"No worries. If you slept like that you needed it. It'll have done you good."

Well, I've certainly got my appetite back. The food shimmered on the sunny table. Fish. Glistening fresh, lightly poached. Of course. What an island this was for fish. Wonderful salads. Marta heaped her plate. And there were strawberries glowing from the dessert trolley, surrounded by yellow mounds of fresh cream. Sometimes she could understand Alan's passion for coming here. Even admit that he'd rather live here than Manhattan. But surely their child – children – should grow up in the heart of things?

Maura McNeale must be some kind of genius at finding and keeping staff in this remote place. Even those strong, freckled hands, couldn't do half the work here. Perhaps the girls helped out sometimes.

She was bustling about now, clearing plates from tables.

"Were you born in Australia, Mrs. McNeale? This fish is lovely, by the way." Marta's compliment was genuine. The fish was always lovely on the island. Always fresh.

"Yes. Aussie born and bred." Maura laughed. "My parents came from Poland though. You know, the usual thing. The war. They had to leave. And they finally made it to Australia. Had a hard time too – out in the Snowy Mountains at first. But they settled down. Never left anyway."

Ah, from Poland. I'm never wrong about people.

"They were from the Tatra mountains, your parents?"

Maura put the soup tureen down, and stared at her. "Why, yes. However did you know that?"

"Your house, this restaurant, it just said The Tyrol to me from the moment I walked in. And the Tatra mountains is the Tyrolean part of Poland right?"

"Well, most people wouldn't even know that, never mind where my parents came from. And you're right. Mama often talked about how lovely the mountains were. In a way I think she was almost sorry to leave the Snowies for Perth. She'd have felt right at home here."

Maura was now clearing other tables.

I am a late luncher. The last. How long was I asleep? The water was so warm in that pink bath. The sprigged air filled pillow so soft. As if the air was softer at this altitude!

I think it's your brain that's softening with pregnancy Marta; but not so that you couldn't place Maura anyway.

Alan had said, with his usual fond pride: "Marta is one of those rare people who can understand figures and people. Both halves of her brain are fully functioning."

It did seem to be either/or with a lot of people. Some of her most brilliant colleagues seemed almost autistic when it came to people.

Marta stared out of the window, glad to be alone to think. And to feel a silent companionship in the recent presence of other diners. The trees, heavy with their summer green, had blurred the Southland sky. Its clarity of blue, its new washed clouds – had disappeared – soaked up by the new green of summer.

The lush lawn, bordered by a stained-glass edging of flowers, swept up to the wall of forest. There was a little blonde girl in the distance, playing with her father. Who was blonde like her. And tall.

Seeing the child, the schoolgirl Carmel came vividly to Marta. They used to walk home together from school. Carmel so fair, she so dark, in their bottle green uniforms, under the heavy chestnut trees.

Daddy was there then. Mum, at home in the kitchen, bustling. Be quiet girls, don't bother your daddy, he's had a hard day. But he never minded. He always had time for play.

He could work all day. And play all night

Marta watched father and daughter playing in the rainforest clearing. Yes. Alan would love a daughter. Simply love one. I ought to face that squarely. He might even prefer… if we are only to have one.

It's just that David Alan, two years from now, would fit so well with the life I want. We want.

Now the child was picking flowers. Daisies – or the rainforest equivalent – from the mossy lawn. And her father was teaching her to daisychain.

"Emily! Emily!" An unseen mother was calling them in.

Emily.

A pretty name, for a pretty child. Emily.

But… No. If they were to have this baby, she wouldn't be Emily. Victorian names have had their day I think. Well, Marta smiled over her strawberries, had their day and had their revival. Also it doesn't shorten well. Who wants an Em?

Not Emily then.

Laughing the blond father snatched his daughter into his arms and swung her up to curly tree ferns. "Bigger than at home, Em". They disappeared from Marta's view, pulled by the unseen voice.

I must think things through. I must. But I'm so tired. What

I want is to sleep. An afternoon nap! That is so ridiculous. The thought was swallowed up in a yawn.

I've wasted a whole morning. Just wasted it. I must have been in that bath for hours. Wasn't there something about the colour pink? It was supposed to have a tranquillising effect? They put it in jails or asylums?

Well, it wasn't a colour that would appear in Marta and Alan's Manhattan flat anyway. Unless in a very deep and dusty and disturbing mode.

Suddenly Marta could see the view from the new flat clearer than the rainforest view from the window. Simon had taken her round. To show her what the offered salary would buy.

It would buy them long light rooms, with picture windows that would dwarf these. And a view across that exciting glowing city.

And, if I do well – No, when I do well, because I will – Alan and I can buy another small flat in central London. He, we, can still spend time there.

But it seemed remote now. London had paled beside Manhattan. And the dramatic scenery of the island. But it'll always be home for Alan, face that Marta.

Would a corner of old England work in NY? Perhaps rather darkly paneled rooms. Upholstered furniture. In very carefully chosen chintzes. Vast comfy chairs and sofas that you could sink into…

Marta jerked upright. If I'm going to fall asleep over my coffee, I might as well do it properly.

And what am I doing indoors, lingering over the remains of lunch when there is bright sunshine on that inviting lawn? When there's a lounger on that mossy terrace just waiting for me?

I'll take an hour out. Soak up some sun. Who knows, poor Alan might be back by then, although Maura had said it would probably take him all day. Father and daughter had long gone, walking through Summer forest. So heavy and green. How it sighed and rustled and soothed.

If only I hadn't been so sharp. He would have waited and we could have found this together.

Marta closed her eyes. But the image of Emily stayed on her lids. He would love a daughter, I know. I admit it. But, but, but… We can only have one child. Or what is to happen to my career. And not now. Not just now.

And if we have Emily, do I have to give up David Alan?

There wouldn't be room for one child in their place in London – never mind two.

There was no garden. Not even a balcony. And the traffic rustled along outside the windows all day and all night. The children sighed sadly around her. There'd be acres of space for them in Manhattan and perhaps even that wonderful Central Park right outside the window. The central heating would be more efficient in NY too.

Marta hugged herself against the chill of a London autumn. Surely it was time for the central heating to kick in?

Shivering, she looked up into rustling trees, and few gold leaves floated gently down to her.

The shadows were long on the lawn. Late afternoon and chilly.

I must have slept all afternoon too!!

If this is pregnancy, I don't think I can handle it.

There was no one about. Just Winter stalking her somewhere out there. Marta hurried inside, to the warm safety of the Rainy Day House. Now she really would do some work. There was a library. And computers. The information superhighway here. Fantastic. I can book the tickets, I can even think about those figures. It would be good to get those loose ends tied up. And I can check with the bookshop and make sure that Alan has really put it on the market. At a proper price.

The library was of darker pine. Warm and still. Enormous windows looked out at the gleaming reds and golds of Autumn.

Marta sat in the window seat, watching the leaves fall. This is the season that Alan loves. He says it has such a beautiful sadness about it. But remember Alan, from Manhattan, we shall go to New England in the Fall. Isn't that the Autumn of Autumns?

So I really am not depriving him of anything. He will love New York. So many doors will open to him.

"It's always beautiful, doesn't matter what the season." Mrs. McNeale's bustlings had led her back to Marta again, as she cleared up scattered coffee cups. "I often think that the rainforest is what God put on the earth to show us how to do it. It's so designed, so sculptured. Could you improve a curve of it? Or a line?"

She had a point. I couldn't make one design change that would improve anything. An odd thing to say though. It was the sort of thing Alan would say.

Alan, where are you? Its time you came back to me?

Leaves were drifting and blowing, in the shadows of the late afternoon. Against the massive perma green of the forest, some trees now stood skeletal.

How lovely the forest is, darkening at the end of the day, the end of the year. It seems to go on forever. Dark and deep.

Wasn't that a line from a poem vaguely remembered from school days?

There's another little girl out there. She's having a last play. Before the darkness. How I remember that. With Carmel. My big sister. On Autumn evenings, when the air was heavy with bonfires. We wanted to stay outside as if to catch the very last of the year.

This child was like an autumn leaf, in her rust coloured wool jumper; her tiny patchwork skirt in reds and golds.

A little girl would be such fun to dress, you can't get away from that. And she would be lovely. As this one is. Skimming across the lawn, her doting father in hot pursuit.

He wasn't young; his once gold autumnal hair had the hues of winter in it. And he doesn't look like a stranger at all.

The thought died away, in another yawn.

Such a pretty little girl. The mother was obviously Asian. The child had a perfect pale gold skin, slightly slanting black eyes and inky black hair falling straight round her enchanting face.

"The child of his old age, and very much a treasure." Maura's voice startled Marta, for all its quietness. They stood watching father and daughter play for a while, whirling round and round with the fast falling leaves.

"The forest is still so green though."

"It's always green, with all our Rainy Days", Maura said. 'He loves the rainforest, the green, the seasons, everything."

"They're regular guests then?" Marta asked politely

"Well, he has been coming here for many years. He bought his first wife here once. And then he came back, year after year. So faithfully. I think he always hoped… It's hard, not to know, never to know… He loved her very much. Then, one

51

year Mai was here… lonely too. Her husband had died soon after they married. He was much older than her. And they had Emily."

Another Emily.

Well, that settled it. Whatever name her daughter had. If there was to be a daughter. It would not be Emily. Not if that was what everyone was calling their child. David Alan would have been James Alan, if James hadn't been quite so popular.

"It's really too dark to read. The days are so short now." Maura bustled companionably around. Lighting lamps in the dark corners of the rooms. There was a hum of conversation coming from the bar. And a smell of cold.

Yes. The lawn was empty, and the approaching darkness would soon swallow up the library and the Rainy Day House.

Alan, please get here soon. I miss you so much. After only one day.

"I've put you in the white bedroom."

It must be Bedtime. What a comforting word that was suddenly.

I'll go to sleep – no problems with that today. And when I wake up, Alan will be here.

At least she hasn't put me in the Pink room, Marta thought, as she drifted dreamily along behind her hostess.

Up the wooden stairs to bedlington. She could just imagine Maura saying that.

And what a charming room. Cosy, not cold. It wasn't really white at all.

The pine paneling was darker here. Dark and warm. The bedlinen was snowy, spotless. So downy and comfortable.

The pine bedside table held a light. A Bible. A glass of water. And an alarm clock.

A Tyrolean touch that, thought Marta, amused. No lotus-eating here then. We will all get up brisk and early for a hearty breakfast and then out into the woods. To ski. To walk the glacier.

Maura was at the curtains now looking out before their final closing. The light streamed from the window and died in the black curly forest.

The woods were full of snow, heavy with it. Glowing out of darkness. How sleepy she was. Just to curl up in clean bedlinen, snowy sheets, downy duvets and sleep and stop thinking.

"You have everything you need". Maura closed the door quietly.

"Isn't that usually posed as a question?" thought Marta dreamily. "Why are you so sure I have everything I need, Tyrolean lady?" She snuggled into the duvet. Old-fashioned, heavy, duck down. But with the sweet smell of fresh well aired linen.

Could you hang washing out in the rain forest then? She laughed. She could see Maura doing it. Though perhaps not now. With the snow. Really, truly, deep and crisp and even.

So I have all I need, do I? Maybe. But not all I want. Because I want it all.

And aren't I entitled to want it all? I want me and Alan. I want my Manhattan job. I want my wonderful career. I want to soar to heights undreamed of in those horrible early office days. I want David Alan. Very much. And, yes, maybe I even want little Not-Emily. And I want no more rain forest holidays. It's going to be sun and white sand for us from now on.

I'm sure I know what the Futures hold. I always have. But what does my future hold?

Apparently I have all the information I need.

But I'm so sleepy. It's hard to think with ducksdown beckoning.

What do I have before me?

Me, and Alan, and Not-Emily? Or only the certainty of a long and dreamless sleep?

* * *

Author's note: The poem at the start of *The Rainy Day House* was sent to the Oban Times in early 2013 by a "visitor to Scotland". It has since been printed in blogs about Scotland but I have been unable to find the poet's name.

Klook and Plukey

"Annie! Annie McDonald. It can't be!"

Nice one, Klook, I thought. You've learnt a bit since our schooldays. Pretend I was so insignificant you can't even remember my name.

"Anita, Ann. Anita McDonough." Klook and I stared at each other.

Although just about everyone in our class was called Ann if they weren't called Mary, she wasn't really Ann any more than I was. Her name was Anya. Anya Elizabeth Klook – always known as Klook for some reason. I don't know why. It's not as if we were a public school with our Whartons and our Bunters. We were a Catholic Convent High School "for young ladies". In a drab northern city.

Well, it's quite a trendy city now, to my surprise.

It certainly wasn't trendy in my day. And it wasn't anywhere I intended to stay. Every class had its stars – and I was one of them. And, as far as I'm concerned, I'm a star to this day. Have you ever seen a Sixties compilation album that didn't include me?

Which is why I assumed Klook was faking it. Had learnt a bit of subtlety since our Convent days. She wasn't noted for it then. She was a girl who got physical. I can vividly remember a bruise I got from her long, strong, pinching fingers, just because of something I said to that idiotic Plukey.

But as we settled in the kitchen of her Clapham terrace clutching mugs of coffee, she seemed the same direct old Klook she had always been.

"Anita McDonough! They said the interviewer would be a Kate Moore. I never connected it with you for a moment. I mean how could I have?"

Anita Catherine McDonough, that was me, three marriages ago. You will know me as Kate Dancer; but Mrs. Clifton G. Mohr is who I am officially. Although Cliff and I are now separated.

I've given up arguing about the spelling. Kate Moore sounds good doesn't it? And somehow right for a journalist. Which I am. Or I will be, after this. Don't let anyone tell you different.

Klook sat back, her sharp grey eyes taking me in. Not saying whether she was pleased it was me or not.

"Of course, you were Kate when you were with that Group, the… the…"

I was annoyed that she was genuinely searching for it. I'm being absolutely frank here – after all, who is going to see an unedited version of this? – but I truly did think that she would be one of the girls who would have remembered me vividly. They would all remember me. But Klook… And Plukey!

We were such a contrast. Don't tell me it didn't rankle.

I was so perfectly suited to the Sixties you can't imagine. If you were to have cast me then, you would have had to find a cross between Julie Christie and that girl Samantha, from Top of the Pops, who married a Monkee. Micky Dolenz.

That's how Sixties I was.

My teens and early twenties were heaven. Everyone must have wanted to be me.

But they can't have been a happy time for Klook though. She was as tall and bony as Plukey was… I was going to say fat, but I think squat would be more correct.

Being tall was not the thing in the Sixties. And Klook looked old, not like a schoolgirl at all. The tip of her long, strong nose was always a little bit red.

Even her being so blonde didn't help. She had no eyebrows to speak of, no visible eyelashes. And her hair was sparse and wispy.

She was the exact opposite of a dolly bird. And she didn't help her cause any by hanging around with Plukey.

As for what happened that summer term in the Sixth… . She was supposed to have gone on to University too. That was a big thing in her family.

It must have been traumatic. They talk about the permissive Sixties. But they weren't really. Not in our hometown. That all came later.

I never saw her after that. Though I did hear the baby was a boy, and that Kevin was whisked out of town by his horrified parents.

And one thing she hadn't said to me was: "How long is it since we last saw each other?" All the others had said it straight off,

So I was wondering how and when I should broach that. Perhaps better get the more recent stuff done first.

Oddly, her looks weren't so bad for the nineties. She was rangy now, rather than tall and awkward. Her legs were long and slender in tight jeans. Even the faded blonde hair looked right. It's unfair really, how types come and go.

If you were casting her now, you could use Sheila Hancock. But it wouldn't have worked at all when she was young.

You could never have cast Plukey. Well why would you want to? And time certainly hadn't worked any miracles with her. We had a long and boring interview back in my good old home town some weeks ago.

Now I am still dolly bird in appearance, and if that sounds ridiculous at fifty, take my word for it, it isn't if it's well done. I'm always stylish of course – there is nothing of the oldest-dolly-in-town about my appearance.

"You look just the same, Anita, it's amazing, " Klook chimed in, as if she had read my thoughts.

I smiled carefully, not returning the compliment. Well, in her case, it wouldn't be a compliment.

"It's a long time since our schooldays, Anne" I said, neutrally, wondering exactly what her achievements were compared to mine. After all I was the class star – and still am.

OK. She has written this book, "The Myth of the Permissive Classroom.".

She's Anya Smith now. Dr. Anya Smith! In the unlikely event that you want to read it. It is (apparently) a witty defence of some of the innovations of that time.

It doesn't interest me. I'm here for the softer Sixties angle – to talk about her own childhood, her own schooling.

It's not that I don't have children, I must quickly say that. I think children are very important.

You see, if I hadn't had any, I could have come across as rather pathetic. You know, I have my fame, but I never had the husband and the kiddies that mean real happiness.

But none of the duller of my old classmates can hug themselves over that. Because I do have children. Well, in fact I only have one, my daughter, Sarah or Sally.

Isn't that a good name? It hasn't lost its quality at all.

Of course, she is called Sal, or Sals by everyone. Not me though. Strictly Sarah or Sally.

As I can be absolutely frank here, I can admit that Sal suits her well enough.

She is the true daughter of her father. Leo Dancer. Leo Dancer and the Dancettes. You can't have forgotten us!. Also known as, Leonard Stanley Whelkstone. Not that I knew that.

It was my agent's match in a way. He thought an engagement would be good publicity for our next single. He didn't expect it to go as far as marriage. Alan Miller was our manager then, and the money pretty well ended up being his too.

It's odd that the nuns didn't teach us how to handle money.They were good enough at extracting it from our parents.

Although the engagement was Alan's idea of a good career move, I won't deny that I wanted it as well. You have to remember that in the Sixties, in our town anyway, it didn't do to get to twenty without at least an engagement ring on your finger.

I can remember Leo and I choosing that ring together even now. It was one of the happiest days of my life. Any of the other Dancettes would have been only too happy to be wearing it. Believe you me. I only wish that it could have happened a year earlier and I could have gone back for my last term with it on my finger.

It won't be easy for you to understand what status that could convey.

The ring was the thing then. Almost any man would do frankly. But Leo was gorgeous too. And famous!

If you were to have cast him, I think perhaps Lionel Morton of the Four Pennies would have been right. Nowadays it would have to be Pete Beale from Eastenders.

That's who he was anyway. I don't mean the actor who played him. I mean Pete Beale, the character. That's who Leo Dancer really was.

Anyway, reader, I married him. My glamorous London star. To the horror of Alan Miller, who had only sanctioned an engagement.

And of course I married from the provinces into the provinces, but I didn't realise till it was too late.

"Are you interviewing everyone in our class? Everyone?" Klook brought me sharply back to my duties.

"Oh yes. It's to show the background you were writing from – from the personal experiences of the class of 1966."

"You know, that could work." Klook seemed quite impressed.

I told you I was a journalist, but I don't think you believed me.

"That is, as many as I can find. None of us seem to have died. Well, except Margaret Mary Torcello. She was a nun you know." A fate worse than death anyway, in my opinion.

A lot were still in our hometown. To my surprise. But not all. "Do you remember Maria Kozak?" I asked Klook, cutting off her enquiries and exclamations about Margaret Mary.

"Maria Kozak. Yes, yes I do. Maria. Yes, pretty girl, curly hair, big blue eyes? What my mother would have called "a Chocolate Box Beauty." Klook laughed. – a typical plain-girl reaction that. "She had a wonderful voice didn't she. Any decent school system would have provided her with…"

I interrupted Klook quickly – I did not want to get into her theories of education in any way shape or form – and reminded her that Maria had married into American showbusiness.

"No. Maria? Really? You have been doing your research."

Klook, you should have known about Maria. But I know why you didn't, and perhaps this is going to get me into an area …

"Yes, don't you remember all the excitement at school? Our last year in the sixth? She came in with that beautiful engagement ring. And she told us how she and Ben met. Backstage. She said it was just like West Side Story, when Tony and Maria's eyes meet across a crowded room. It truly was love at first sight? They were married three months later. It made the nuns so mad. You can't have forgotten that wedding!"

And you haven't forgotten Klook. You weren't there to remember any of this, as you, who should have been trying for your Oxbridge admission, were presumably in some gruesome Catholic mother and baby home.

Or were you? All sorts of rumours had gone round. She had had an abortion in London – and died. Or had survived, but terribly changed. The baby had been adopted. The baby was in fact Mr.O'Connell's, and not Kevin's at all!

We never found out. The Klook family disappeared, permanently. And Kevin vanished for long enough.

There were even rumours that Klook and Kevin had been married quickly and quietly in London.

That's one I never believed. And it was disproved anyway, by Kevin's quiet reappearance, engagement and marriage to the respectable, blonde scion of a Catholic Family who were big in the building trade.

But now I was going to find out.

However, Klook poured us another coffee and didn't pick up on my cue. "They're now divorced right?"

Well, Klook, no need to be so waspish just because you will never know love at first sight.

"They were married nearly twenty years and had four boys.

They split up when she was forty and she went to NY and now has this marvellous career in the networks. Maria Fontenot she is now."

Marvellous career is stretching it a bit. She has a job with them. But I wasn't having Klook downgrading any kind of showbiz success.

Maria's faint fame seemed nicely ancillary to my own – I think of her as a kind of bridesmaid to my career.

"Four boys", Klook marvelled. And thus, having avoided my first trap, stepped right into the next one. As I said, I am a journalist. Dolly-bird exterior notwithstanding.

"I thought it would be you to have the four boys Kloo… Anya, Weren't you always Jo of "Little Women"? You were going to have loads of boys weren't you – at least four?" I laughed in what I hoped was a fond reminiscent way.

Klook laughed. Ruefully. I could say, except I think I'll have to find a better word than that. "No, that was my dream. I still think it was a good dream too. But schoolgirl dreams don't really come true. Probably they shouldn't. Well except in Marianne's case of course."

Oh, no, Klook, it was my dreams that came true. Not Marianne Pluckton's.

Certainly not Marianne Pluckton's.

Anyway, I happen to have interviewed Marianne already. Marianne Margaret Pluckton. Although I'm afraid she will always be Plukey to me. So don't try to pretend to me that her dreams came true. Nightmares maybe!

You were always a watchdog for her weren't you Klook? Don't think for a moment I've forgotten that livid bruise on my arm. And, yes, that pathetic girl did have dreams.

I can remember even now the moment she suddenly

changed. We would have been sixteen at the time. It was in Miss O'Donnell's French class.

By the way, she is no longer Marianne Pluckton! She did get married – to a guy we called the X-Ray. Raymond Chandler. I know you aren't going to believe this, but he really was called Raymond Chandler. Raymond Martin Chandler. He would simply be called a Wimp nowadays. But we called him the X-Ray. At least Anne Goss did. She was another girl who just wasn't suited to the Sixties, and her tongue became sharper and sharper as the terms went by.

I don't know what happened to her. She named the X-Ray and disappeared.

It was his name alright. His face was thin and one dimensional. And he was a peevish, whining type.

Still, he did have a good surname. Chandler is infinitely better than Whelkstone. If Plukey's dream was to get a better surname, she certainly achieved it. I very nearly said that out loud. I needed to get us back to the subject of children.

"Yes, I went down to see Marianne last month. I spent the day at her house."

And a long day it had been too. She has not changed. Just got older, squatter and dustier looking. She kept asking me questions – who I married, where I live now, children, grandchildren. She never asked about my career though. Not surprisingly. She had stayed at home with the kids, plus done a bit of teaching in our old school!

Can you get drearier than that? But oddly enough she is the one who seems to have kept up with people, or at least who knows where they are.

It was she who told me about Maria. And Klook. But even she didn't know where Anne Goss or Emily Plant were.

Klook said with a few more disappearances we might have the material for a local "Picnic at Hanging Rock". I must say that I would love to cast the Me character.

Klook didn't know where anyone was really, except for Plukey, but Plukey had a ton of addresses. So I had to see her.

But I had to work for the information. Not only did I have to answer all those questions – as briefly as possible by the way, I wasn't going to waste the wonderful crafted version I have of my life on Plukey – but I had to do the tour of the house.

That was dreary too. New, on one of those boring estates – you know, 4 bed, 2 bath, utility room. I had to look at innumerable albums full of photos of children and grandchildren.

I even had to lunch with the X-Ray, who comes peevishly home at noon every day. It turns out that he is a wizard with computers.

Which seems appropriate. Computer Nerd fits him exactly. Most middle aged husbands are thrilled to have someone as glitzy as me around. They usually flirt with me like mad. But not the X-Ray, of course. I just felt that I interfered with his whining as peevishly through lunch as he would have liked.

Anyway, I'd got that interview behind me. Thankfully. And it had given me all the basic contacts I needed. And it even seemed to have warmed Klook up to me as she was suddenly telling me how lovely it was of me to spend a day with Marianne and how pleased she must have been.

Actually, if I was anything at all to Marianne Pluckton, I'm sure I was a galling reminder of all the things she could never be. However, if it had made Klook happy….

"Yes, I spent a day with Marianne and Ray. Their daughter, Celia, was visiting with the baby so I met her as well."

That was no pleasure either. Celia has all the social graces of her father, and the baby grizzled the whole time.

"Celia, yes, she's so pretty isn't she?"

Well. No. I wouldn't say "so pretty". But they are strange things, genes. Plukey's daughter looked just like her father, but with Plukey's sulky, sullen mouth. Yet, somehow, the effect was of a fragile, graceful sexiness.

They also had a son. A male version of Plukey, but fortunately with his father's height. He's a computer nerd too.

He's married to a Thai girl. I had to see all the wedding photos. Then the children, from babyhood on. But they were enchanting. Two little girls.

So Plukey had three granddaughters, which she went on and on about, and apparently the daughter-in-law is expecting again, and they are all hoping for a boy this time.

Well, she has certainly got prettier grandchildren than she and her X-Ray are entitled to, but none so lovely as my Freddie.

"Have you got any children, Anita?" At last. The question I wanted. Because if I show you mine, you can show me yours. Anyway, I found I was eager to tell Klook the official version of my life, the one I hadn't bothered to waste on Plukey.

I'd just given her the blunt truth when she asked the same question. Yes. One. A daughter. Brought up by her granny.

That's my ex-mother in law, Annie Whelkstone. All nudging elbows and ear splitting. screeching about winkles. The Whelkstone Harem were expected to be all-girls-together in the kitchen, wherever we were. You can be sure that I was a great disappointment to them. Annie was openly thrilled that I left Leo so quickly, and even more thrilled when he finally married the kind of shrieking blonde so dear to the Harem's heart. And she was only too happy to take Sarah in the interim.

Which was a good thing, as there is no way my own mother would have helped.

You Made Your Bed, You Lie On It. That was her motto. She couldn't wait for me and my sister to leave home. She had us weaned and potty trained almost before she left the maternity ward.

As for my next husband… The less he knew about my Whelkstone life the better. His baronial hall awaited the Sloanish sons he now has.

I didn't choose to linger in that marriage I can tell you. And I did not like the way the tabloids handled it. Just because Charles comes across like such a dreamboat, everyone always supposes he must have left me. As if I would let myself get into that sort of relationship! That's for the Klooks of this world.

There we all were, trying to walk the tightrope of fifties femininity, the sixties beginning to make it sway dangerously. And here were clumsy Klook and squat Plukey trying to clamber aboard.

They had to be shaken off, for all our sakes. Surely even they must have seen that?

Of course, Klook fell off before we even knew she was trying.

But Plukey… Cleverness was all she had. And she deliberately gave it away to be one of us. To be one of the ones giggling in groups about boyfriends. To be in the engagement ring competition. To join in those discussions about solitaire diamonds or emeralds, or maybe a sapphire cluster. Perhaps she even wanted to join the countdown. What stage did you get to last night…? One, two, three? Anything over a five was considered a bit beyond the pale.

Can you imagine Plukey? Anyway, I saved us from that. I saved her from that. Though it earned me a Klookian pinching.

Plukey, that dull, squat class swot, had been bouncing around us all week, suddenly unable to conjugate a verb, or work out a theorem to save her life. Miss O'Donnell, usually so mild, was furious with her.

And giggling! Plukey – Giggling!! It was horrible. Embarrassing. Going on about a boy who had asked her out. Help, girls, what should she do?

"You should get back in your shell, Marianne", I said sharply and truthfully, "It suits you much better in there."

I didn't know that Klook was lurking behind the next coat rack, or I wouldn't have risked saying it.

My arm was sore for days.

And why should Klook have tried to make me feel guilty about it?

She was in the wrong. Not me.

Getting physical like that! Girls didn't get physical then.

We had our weapons. But we kept our knives under our tongues.

Anyway I knew I was right. She was never going to bully me into seeing things her weird way. I was doing Plukey a favour. And Marianne Pluckton knew it as well as the rest of us.

Because after that she shut up, and stopped embarrassing

herself and the rest of us. She didn't go back to being clever though.

She was quieter and more sullen than ever. Didn't answer in class any more.

And don't go blaming me. It was just that Klook disappeared shortly after that. So then Marianne had to sit on her own at lunchtime. And all the teachers got so mad at her – seeing both their Oxbridge hopes disappearing.

"Another pretty girl!" That was Klook gushing over my photos of Sarah. I'd got to that point in my story.

I glide rather neatly over my second disastrous marriage, by worrying about how the divorce affected my child. But – look! – she has turned out fine. And here are the photos to prove it. Then I can get on to my marriage to Cliff. He was so famous then even Klook will remember him.

You'll remember him too. Surely? Clifton G.Mohr – he was the D.A. in Blick Ford. He always started off opposing Blick, but coming over to the right side in the end. It was a relief to be married to someone so much older than me, who just adored me as I was. He had no family over here. And no baronial halls to fill. He left his American wife and the four kids for me. They got all the loot though, as I found out too late.

Still, he was a lovely guy, until he started to go on and on about his family, and guilt, and then the drinking took over.

I've found that with all men really. They start off nice and gorgeous, but it doesn't last.

Anyway, we were at the photograph stage, and probably not going to get as far as Cliff. But I was happy to leave it there. Because my Sarah is more than pretty. She is stunningly photogenic, like her mum. In her photographic form, she's a real credit to me.

"Oh! And two pretty granddaughters as well! And the little grandson. He is a darling." Klook was now admiring my "grandchildren" picture.

Marianne picked up on that straight away. She realised the two girls must be Sarah's stepdaughters. Which indeed they are.

In fact I had to send up a silent prayer that Klook wasn't going to ask me their names, as I realised I couldn't remember them.

The little boy, Freddie, is Sarah's. So I do have a grandchild Scott Frederick Whelkstone. I had to fight hard for that Frederick, and he is always Freddie to me. She had him when she was seventeen, and I have no idea who the father is. I only hope that she does. At any rate, he has never paid a new pence piece towards his son's upbringing.

"I've just got the one grandson." Klook was turning to her battered kitchen dresser to get the usual photos when the door flew open, a little blonde boy hurtled in, and the photos were rendered unnecessary.

I looked at him quickly and carefully. He was about seven, so, if this was Klook's one grandchild, this must be the grandchild of Kevin. He was a standard issue small boy – about seven. Nothing of the young Kevin about him at all. Not nearly as lovely as my Freddie.

Believe me. That's true, not just a fond grandmother talking. I never compromise in my assessment of looks. Freddie is as photogenic as me and Sarah put together.

Kevin was gorgeous too. He was the son of Mr. O'Connell the Science Teacher at the Boys equivalent of our High School for Young Ladies. Who was something of a heart-throb himself.

If you were casting Kevin, it would have had to have been Dirk Bogarde as he appeared in his earliest films. The young Terence Stamp would have done too, but with his hair and eyebrows as dark as dark.

He filled all our daydreams. Except the tough girls like Anne Goss or Klook, who sneered at our helpless addiction. Which made it even more astonishing when Klook proved to be the one who had fallen all the way for his charms.

Or perhaps it wasn't so astonishing. What else would Klook have to offer him? You see the Rule in the early Sixties was this: Pretty girls didn't have to. And plain girls were fools if they did.

So if you were hopelessly plain and willfully foolish in these tightrope matters, well… The result was inevitable.

"Go and say hello to Anita, Ben.,She was at school with mummy. A long time ago."

Benjamin. Yes, that's a good name. I'll give Klook that. And it shortens well.,Freddie just has the edge though, don't you think?

I smiled my most glamorous smile and Ben did linger for a few minutes chatting about his computer, before he somersaulted out of the door and into the garden.

I often think that motherhood could have been very different for me if I had had a son.

Then it suddenly registered on me that Klook had said "mummy" not "gran".

Which startled the incautious exclamation "Ben's YOURS!" out of me.

Klook laughed. "I know, I know. I am a somewhat elderly mum. We thought he was an early menopause actually. It was quite a shock. But a very welcome one. We'd always wanted children. I'd felt so bad I couldn't give Jim any. You know, after Kevin was born, I got this terrible infection. I'm sure it was that place. They treated us like dirt certainly."

I sat there, not following up. She had called him Kevin. She had had Kevin's child. A son. And called him Kevin. Kevin. Anyway did that hack it as a name now? Only if you weren't a Catholic surely....

Fortunately, Klook was answering some of the questions I should have asked. "It was where I met Jim though. That place. He was painting and decorating. Always under an armed guard of nuns. For his own sake, you'll realise. We were a home full of very depraved young schoolgirls indeed. One day he winked at me. And I winked back. And when he went back to London, I went with him. My poor parents were torn between horror at a Registry Office Wedding. To a Protestant!! In London!! and sheer relief that I would never be out there, unprotected, with their first grandson. Poor things. You don't realise what you put your parents through till you have kids of your own."

Unfortunately, I wasn't listening as closely as I should have been, and probably missed some vital details.

Kevin! Would you have called him Kevin in her place? Doesn't it show a certain lack of – I don't know. Something. Then it registered with me that she must have been seventeen when she met this Jim.

"Klook", I blurted out, "You could have won in the engagement ring stakes."

"What?" (She didn't seem to have noticed the Klook.)

"You know. You must have been seventeen when you met Jim. If you'd only been at school, you could have come into class with your engagement ring."

Klook laughed and laughed. "You know, Anita, you're right. I almost could have. On a chain round my neck. And whispered about it during Miss O'Donnell's class when I should have been concentrating on my Oxbridge Entrance. And driven the poor woman insane. She was so good to me, you know. She really begged me not to give up, to try to find a way back. I wrote to her when I did finally get my degree, and thanked her."

As I said, Klook was always seriously weird.

"Can you imagine it, with the baby though! The baby in one arm, the ring in the other. Impossible. Even if I had had him adopted. They tried to make me you know. Not my parents. The Little Sisters of Horribleness. I could have had my Kevin adopted into a severe Catholic home that would have made him feel his shame, and then I could have atoned for my wantoness by joining The Little Sisters. I can't tell you what I used to feel about them. Although, I will admit, we certainly don't have it right nowadays with this completely permissive tolerant attitude. It's a point I want to develop more in the next book…"

I cut in quickly by asking her if that was their wedding picture on the mantelpiece. It obviously was, but I wanted a closer look as well as to shut her up.

She got it down, and we both looked at Klook in a rather drab blue dress and coat beside a fairish youth almost as tall as her.

"I'm not sure he would have passed the Anne Goss test, but I couldn't have married a nicer guy."

So she remembered that too. I suppose we had all been cut by Anne's tongue.

Actually, Jim looked ordinary… Just ordinary. And being

from London would have given him a glamour he most probably didn't deserve. And I should know that, as well as anyone.

No – he would have done fine Klook. We would have thought you had done rather well for yourself. And treated you with a bit more respect. Although, actually, we did treat her with respect, to her face. It was simply too painful not to.

There's an odd fact about these husbands that, as a journalist, I suppose I should note.

It was so important then to get that engagement ring on, to be married, to have the house, the kiddies. It was good to have a gorgeous guy to match the ring of course. That was a real victory.

But in the end, time goes by. So quickly. And then one middle-aged husband is much the same as any other.

Even the X-Ray is just that now. A middle-aged husband. Who provides. Quite well I suppose. And he's certainly faithful. I mean chance would be a fine thing for him!

It's as if you can't keep your trophies.

Klook was hunting through her untidy dresser for photos, but stopped as the front door sounded. "Well, never mind the photos, meet the real thing. Davey!" This to a tiny little dark haired boy who rushed into her arms.

"Meet David, the apple of his old granny's eye. And Davey here's a new Auntie for you. Auntie Anita."

David, rather a darling, bounded into my arms and began to chat away about a furry doggy they had met on the steps outside. And David is one of those names that just always works.

Klook promptly disappeared. Apparently she had been

after that furry doggy and its steaming step presents for some time. My arm throbbed in sympathy for the dog and its owner.

"Do I get a kiss and a cuddle from this glamorous new Auntie too?" I looked up to find a young man who could only be Klook's Kevin gazing down at me admiringly.

And what a charmer he turned out to be! He looks like his mum really – and those sort of looks aren't bad on a guy – but he has all the charm of his father.

And he has Kevin the First's eyes. A luminous hazel, that look almost green in some lights. I had forgotten the tender, melting power of those eyes. The way they looked at you, and only you.

He was thrilled to meet me, and couldn't hear enough about the show biz life. And Klook sat benevolently by, mainly occupied with young David, and his drawings of the naughty doggy.

In fact Kevin and I had quite a tete-a-tete, as Klook, typically, made a vivid drawing of something very unpleasant steaming on her front steps, that had Davey in such fits that he had to be taken off to the garden to recover.

"Well", said Kevin the Second benevolently as we watched them disappear "Mother will grow up one of these days. So you were at school with her. I just can't believe it. I had no idea they had anyone so famous in the class."

Isn't that typical of Klook? Not even to have mentioned me.

I longed to say to him. I knew your father too. I went out with him once. And more than that. I saw him just recently. And his wife. Would she count as a step-mum or not? And your half sister.

Did he know? Had he ever met Kevin the First?

If he hadn't, perhaps he shouldn't meet him now. He has not worn well. He has the puffy face of the heavy drinker, and his hands shake. He is married to Mary Kandarski (as was) – a hatchet faced blonde who was in the year below us. She runs her own riding school and has turned into one of those loud voiced, weather-beaten women who move everywhere with an entourage of horsey little girls in tow.

The first Kevin has a seat on the board at Reilly Kandarski though. Which is something Klook could never have provided.

I was still mulling it all over when Klook returned and Kevin and his little son left. And, believe it or not, she and I sat there all afternoon, talking about our shared past.

And I'm sure you know by now that I do not usually waste my time sitting around in kitchens talking to the girls.

I have no time for all this girly-gang stuff. You know, a girl's best friend is her best girl friends. That's the in-idea now, isn't it?

It's Whelkstone Harem Chic! Who could have believed it?

But the hours just flew by in Klook's kitchen. We talked over old times. Its strange how you forget. The names of the nuns. The smell of polish, the shining wooden floors. The bleak toilets. I could almost smell school dinners at one point.

Is that a smell that's vanished, along with everything else from my youth?

Don't they have canteens now, with multiple choice menus?

And it came to me sharply in Klook's kitchen, for the first time, that my youth really has gone. Vanished – like the wind that swept through Tara!

Or was it Georgia?

Klook has invited me back, you know. Anytime. And, to my surprise, I would like to see her again.

The whole afternoon threw such an interesting light on our shared schooldays.

I hadn't realised just how funny some of the nun-things were.

It was as if we were looking back through a kaleidoscope that Klook was turning, and all sorts of interesting new patterns were beginning to emerge.

But then, being Klook, she just had to administer a final pinch, at the front doorstep, as we waved goodbye.

We had exchanged email addresses, that sort of thing, and I had arranged to get the transcript of the interview to her. And she had even promised me that I would be first to hear about the new book.

And, then, as I began to walk to my taxi she called out: "Thanks again for spending that day with Marianne. You don't know how much she enjoyed it!"

Now what did she mean by that?

Why thank me? She didn't thank me for interviewing Maria or any of the others? Or blame me for not finding the Annes and the Emilys. Why would Plukey have enjoyed our boring day together so much?

Because I'm the most glamorous thing to enter her life since our schooldays?

Probably. Surely that was it?

But as I drove away, the Klookian kaleidoscope began to turn through that day with Marianne, throwing up disturbing new patterns.

She had definitely been pleased to see me. That was true enough. She had shown me round the house with as great a relish as her drab persona can show. As I said, it was the standard new estate 4-bed detached, completely with all the ensuites and utility rooms anyone could require.

It was on an estate in The Village – that's the old part of the town. The "good" part. It amused me that she rather stressed that, as if I might have forgotten.

I had forgotten how green it was there though, and how pretty all the old stone cottages are. The few new estates there all have to be built in stone of course.

She insisted I stay for my lunch with the X-Ray, and for the long afternoon with Celia and granddaughter No.3.

I even had to look at all their Wedding Anniversary Photos. All being the word.

And she asked me so many questions. I don't even remember what I said. Not much. It was only Plukey after all.

So she certainly must have been pleased to see me, for all she was her usual sullen self.

Although, the further I got from Klook's the more the word sullen didn't seem quite right any more, and, if there is such a thing as a psychic arm, mine began to throb.

Her big house. Her long marriage. Her faithful husband. (The X-Ray came with that guarantee). Children. Grandchildren. All her questions, extracting the bare bones of my life so far.

A very different pattern began to emerge as a possibility. Her expression, which I had defined as sullen and sulky, seemed to reform and re-pattern itself, requiring a new definition.

But how to describe it?

The word I'm looking for couldn't possibly be "smug", could it?

* * *

Author's note: When I was getting this collection together, and talking about it with Peter Hiley, an old friend from our college days, I found not only was he also writing about those 1950/60s schooldays, but that we are both on the Aspergers/Autism Spectrum. And the school system being, of necessity, one size fits all, most certainly did not suit us. Nor did we suit it, to be fair.

So I was interested to see how he had written about it. Where I have tackled it obliquely, through a point of view not my own, Peter has chosen to tackle it directly, writing about that dreadful first day, and the lesson we learnt – that we would not fit in, that, at school, we were strangers in a strange land. The following extract is from "Pete's Angel" by Peter Hiley, as yet unpublished, as it is a work in progress.

'Here you are, this is your class, just do what the teacher says and you'll be OK',

Mum looked anxiously at his skinny little body following the line of children going in.

There was a group of little chairs and desks in one corner of a huge echoey hall with high brick walls. The scrabble for seats made a chaotic din that crushed Peter into a pulp. Standing alone and hating to have people looking at him, he took a seat at the back. As he lifted the desk lid to screen himself, the teacher said in a commanding voice, 'Desk lids down please.'

It was like those horrid birthday parties in which he felt like an alien.

His mind wandered, escaping, examining the roof, which was almost flat.

Roofs should have two slopes and a ridge …

... at playtime a group of boys and girls gathered around this strange boy, trying to wind him up, for that is the nature of many children.

'Where do you live?' 'What's your Dad do?' they said apparently quite pleasantly. 'Do you know Incy Wincy?'

Peter knew no songs at all, so he just stood there, shaking, trying not to cry, while they all sang the song AT him.

When they finished, the real taunting started.

'Which team is top of the league?'

'Who's your favourite tennis player?'

'Can you play cowboys and indians?'

'Yew don't know nuffink.'

They started chanting, 'Eggy cheese and tomato,' over and over while he stood there. The duty teacher shooed the baiters away, but the damage had been done. Peter knew he was a stranger in school.

Till They Dropped

'We used to build civilisations.
Now we build shopping malls.' – BILL BRYSON

Emily had been sitting in the plaza for some time, before she heard the rustling. She had been so thirsty after those days in the dead area that all she had thought of was water. The humming booth had churned out ice-cream sodas which she greedily gulped down. She listened – ice-cream soda hands frozen in mid-air – but there was no further sound, only the taped splashing of the fountain.

If she could stay here, frozen in foliage until lightset, surely she could get away somehow. She began to count exits, swiveling her eyes, not moving her head. Over there, the wide green stairs continued down, round the corner.

She had a reluctance to go down. So many of the previous doors had opened on stairs that had gone down. Only those doors were not green, they had been chipped wood or worn stone.

She had been coffined in dead wood. Surely no life could ever have animated the rooms that she had come through. Endless rooms, and stairs, and doors. Enough light to make the shadows come alive, but never enough to see ahead.

No water at all. Not even taps to drip.

She had travelled on – room to room, floor to floor – upwards. She had to get to light. Once, out of darkness, came a rustle and white teeth set in a rocking smile had gleamed beside her. She had run as she didn't know she could run, scrambling through door upon door, in the terrible quarter light.

The fruits she had carried in her jacket hood had kept her alive, but they had been finished, when, half conscious she had come to the room with only one door. That was when the temptation to try to go back had been strongest. The seeming infinity of choices had narrowed down to one small and shabby wooden door, so low she would have to stoop to get through.

They said it was written in the walls that to go back was certain death. So she had opened the rackety door to find stairs, narrow and dark, but going up.

She propped the door open with her jacket, just in case there were no more doors, but it had creaked shut behind her in a dead mechanical way, as if the Mechanism that animated it was at its last gasp.

Now she was in total darkness. But she went on, upwards. Fifty stairs. A hundred. Two hundred. Still there was nothing but darkness above her. The taste of dust and defeat was on her tongue and she knew she must go back. Now. Before the darkness panicked her. Before teeth gleamed beside her.

She would have to go back through that door. She would go back. What else was there to do? She had kept count, and could find it again, two hundred stairs down.

Never ever go back
What Follows will catch
those fools who backtrack.

So never retract
Never ever go back

Light! For a moment the walls glowed with the message. But she had no choice. Down 198 stairs, 199… and there was no door. And the stairs kept on going down.

They couldn't. They didn't. Yet her feet went on down and down, three hundred, four hundred stairs. What follows will catch. She knew that if there was any salvation it was up. These impossible stairs would take her down forever. How long did she clamber back up the staircase, groping in the dark, stopping, sobbing, always striving to keep count.

She beat desperately on the wall. There had been a door, somewhere, sometime. Right here, if her counting was still true.

Something gave, and she was falling. But she was falling through, not down. Falling into light. Brilliant light, then instant darkness.

* * *

Green light and rushing water woke her. She dragged herself into a kneeling position. She was on a green marble balcony. Through marble pillars she could see into a verdant plaza below, with ponds and fountain, a cafe and potted trees.

A mirage. A dream. It would get away. Sobbing, she dragged herself to the rail. It was too far down to jump. She would die here with the sound of water filling her ears. Green marbled walls were to the right of her, behind her, but on the left were wide green marble stairs. There was no bend, no corner. They led straight to the plaza.

There was no door behind her, just a blank marble wall. If branches died, did cauterizing and sealing take place? She shuddered to think how close she might have come to falling with the dying leaf. Onto a dark and haunted forest floor.

Had going back saved her? Cautiously, holding her breath, she crawled down.

Hours later she was still sipping the ice-cream sodas, provided by the humming booth, comfy in cushions and warmed by the rays of the sunlamps. Till the noise – if it was a noise. And the image of a trap, cunningly baited, came to her.

Sitting stilly in the green light, she wondered if she had really thought she could stay here. The booth, so busily humming, would make her snacks of food and cold drinks, one after the other. Until now she had never doubted that the Mechanism was her friend. A seed of death had come into it, but it still fed her, and watered her, and gave her soft things to sleep on.

Was the booth her friend? Or was its activity a signal for something else – a following something? If she really had gone back, then ... What follows will catch?

Night came suddenly. The light switched off and the green fluorescence from the booth was reflected in the water from the pool.

If the following sound came in the night, which exit could she make for? She strained to listen, but could hear nothing. The fountain stopped at lightset. The friendly booth had quietly closed itself and put down its shutters. Could she have spent the night safely inside?

She had considered it. But suppose, in the morning, when she went out through the booth door ... Too late now anyway.

So. The stairs. They went on going down, and they were as green, clean and inviting as ever in so far as could be seen.

A curving arcade led off from beside the booth. But its shops had remained dark and shuttered and it had a troubling deadness about it. The wall behind her was opaque green glass shining eerily in the dark. It disappeared up into the green glass lanterns hung like jungle creepers from … whatever was up there.

In front of her curved walls of palest green marble, also shining very faintly, and right in the middle the straight path, faintly lit, marbled going on into … what?

If the patio was not the trap, then maybe that one inviting corridor would be. It was a long long way down. And she could not run. In spite of the door, the drink, being rested, she could not run.

And she had no food or water and no way of carrying any now. What about the paper cups – her innumerable ice-cream soda cups? Could she fill a couple of those from the fluorescent pool? But the wastebin didn't seem to be there anymore. Silent Cleaners must have swallowed it up.

She simply could not bring herself to go into that dark and curving arcade. Even with the light of the green day shining into it what lay in the shadows beyond the curve had looked not just closed but sinister.

And the broad marble road, that looked so inviting, seemed more and more like a trap. Suppose it had no turnings, no doors. She had stared down in daylight and had been dizzy after a while with the sense of infinite space and had had to look away.

That only left the stairs going down. And did they also have a circular slant towards the dead bit she had escaped from?

But it had been a friendly straightforward staircase that had led her to the humming plaza. And it continued down, wide and comfortable, but curving. She sat and thought a long time, glad not to have to make any decision.

Creak.

The noise came from behind the dark silk bushes masking the entrance to the arcade. Then absolute silence.

Had she heard …? What had she heard?

Was there a rustle in the plants?

Suddenly she was running. She didn't know where she was running until she found herself stumbling, clutching, falling down the glowing green staircase. Round and round it went, round and round her feet went. She was in full light now.

Don't stop. Don't stop. There must be an exit. A door. Just keep going. Spiralling round. Bright green light. Doubled up, a stitch tearing at her side, she had to stop on one of the broad landings. Still the staircase curved above and below. Thank God there was light here.

Teeth beside her in the darkness were a hallucination of darkness, not the light. What had rustled in the silk bushes?

Just Cleaners, she tried to tell herself. Just the Cleaners. But hadn't they already been and gone so silently that she hadn't heard them. Suddenly her body stiffened. A tiny sound had come from the stairs below her.

Something small and light was coming up the stairs. Fast.

Here was the trap then. She had chosen wrong. Panicked into the net. Her feet fast in treacle, she tried to move back up the broad marble stairs. Away from that tiny intense shuffling. But what waited upstairs? The rustler in the bushes?

Frozen with panic, she pressed herself into the cold green wall and watched the bend of the stairs below her. Now she was trapped by the death that had somehow got into their beautiful Mechanism.

Shuffle, shuffle.

Furry paws with little claws came into view. It wanted her. It was loved. It was climbing doggedly up towards her up gigantic steps.

'Teddy!' It was Edward Bear from childhood.

Tears ran down her face as she laughed weakly, waiting for Teddy to change, to reveal the evil eyes and large claws that lurked behind the fluffy disguise.

Don't panic my dear, don't panic, its only old Teddy. Beloved Edward Bear. Come, let me kiss you.

Shark teeth would smile, mouth would approach neck, and loving kisses would suddenly … Paws had grasped her ankles. The light wool paws of childhood. And above her something creaked on the stairs.

'Emily! Hurry.'

How strange to hear that voice outside her head for the first time ever.

'What follows will catch, if we don't hurry.'

'Edward!'

She snatched him up. He had come from somewhere to save her. Now she must save him.

'Edward, the door, the door, where is the door? Any door?'

Now he was a relaxed stuffed toy in her arms.

'Edward, I can't go on. I can't. Where does this staircase go?'

'We don't want to go where this staircase goes. We must go through.'

The strangeness of hearing the voice outside her head – and the strangeness of what it said.

Suddenly he wriggled, swarmed down her, and disappeared head first through the deep tread in the stair below. Amazed, she knelt and pressed at it. It swung in, loose. A teddy-bear flap. How could she get through that?

'Follow me,' still hung in the air . And tappety tap came from the stairs above. Horribly close.

Edward. Don't leave me. I'm not a child anymore. I can't go through that.

But she could go through. If I can then I must be getting smaller … The thought was cut off by a terrible falling, and then they were bouncing together on a kingsize bed, in a vast emporium of beds – a sea of beds, to the far horizons.

'Now, keep still.' Edward became a cuddly toy strewn on the mattress. She lay flat on her back, staring up at the vast space above them, hung with carpets. No opening visible, but somewhere up there. Keep still.

The movement came from way in front of them, a figure in the far distance, moving towards them fast. A Shopper? What if he was a Shopper? She must warn him. No. The figure moved as if on wheels, too fast for anything but a Seller. The Bedseller. He had a hungry, alert look about him. The vast herds of Shoppers were pretty well extinct. His pickings would be slim indeed. And now something had moved in his bed empire.

'Ted, it's OK. I have no credit.'

She had been lost so young. In her first week ever away from home. It had been Freshers' Week, and trailing sadly round the strange, unconnected town, trying to work out how to shop without the Mechanism, she had seen the door – the door to home, to 5 Disraeli Crescent. She had stepped through unhesitatingly, even though the Mechanism was not supposed to be there yet. But the door had taken her ... well, that was a long, long time ago.

The thought 'a long, long time ago' came as a shock. How long, Emily? What have you been doing?

She looked at her small hands. It had been a shock to find that Papa had cut her credit off. At first she thought guiltily that he had found out about her excesses with the new shopping machines. Only later did she come to realise that he was trying to protect her.

'Be quiet, keep still, credit may not matter now.'

Furry Edward taking care of her – she who had been alone for so long. But if credit didn't matter, she must keep very still. A cloak of invisibility had gone from her.

The Bedseller was moving quickly through his vast showroom – a mile or so more and he would be looming, unctuous and ominous, beside them.

Em fought to keep memories out of her mind. When had she last seen Sellers at full throttle? In the carpet bazaar – so attractive and crooked, with a hot, dusty effect to the lighting. She had lived there for a while. Sipping at the cardamom teas and eating the sticky honey pastries. At lightset she had slept, comfy in carpets. She had nested happily there until what she didn't want to think about.

So don't think about it, Emily. Not with a Seller gliding swiftly towards your bed. Think instead about getting home, at last. A sharp movement from the other side of the Bed Empire made her gasp and turn her head.

But it wasn't the Following Thing that had rustled so swiftly in the silk bushes and tapped so fast down the stairs. It wasn't even another Seller. It was simply more beds arriving. The vast lift doors were opening, revealing a tower of brand new mattresses. No wonder the Showroom had expanded so much. All these beds arriving, month after month. And when did they ever sell any?

There had only been one shopper on the Street of the Thousand Carpets. But plenty of carpets, carpets overflowing onto the pavement, carpets clogging up the cardamom coffee booth. And a surplus of Sellers. Nothing had been Closed then. Or had the closures already started and she hadn't noticed? Certainly there had been nothing like the dead area, where only she was alive. And the teeth that smiled out of darkness.

The Bedseller was getting close now. Em looked over at Teddy. Reassuringly he seemed bigger, more furry, more protective. Two more minutes and we'll be OK, said a furry voice, in or outside her head.

'Now.'

Amazingly, Teddy was jumping up. Calling her. And, hand in hand they were walking towards – no they were following the Bedseller.

Of course. Tea break. The big clock on the wall said 10.55. He'd been walking eagerly towards his tea, not towards them. And there was a canteen door quite close. It was the only door in sight. They must have fallen through timeset upon timeset …

Emily was glad to eat and drink again. A frilly Seller glided up to their table and she shrank low on her seat, not even daring to chew, only to jerk back upright again as the next shock hit her.

This was not a Seller.

'Dorabella!'

'Dee. Everyone calls me Dee. I wouldn't answer to

Dorabella anymore than I would dress myself in mustard coloured wool.'

Dorabella – Dee – spat out the words 'Mustard coloured wool' with real scorn.

Emily guiltily remembered knitting that little dress. Perhaps she hadn't been up to mothering someone like her exquisite Dorabella. She appreciated the fact that Edward was much too kind and mature to complain about the eye. She had always meant to sew another button on.

She bit nervously at her doughnut, unable to stop herself glancing round to see if the Sellers would look up from their plastic cakes and cups of painted tea. This canteen was huge, a sea of Sellers surrounded her to the distant horizons. She looked back towards the door they had come through, knowing what she would find. No door. Suppose they realised who or what she was. Em had reason to know just how venomous even two of them could be.

Her sweet, rosy cheeked, chubby Dorabella – Dee – seemed to fit in perfectly. But Dora's clothes … A vague alarm bell rang in Em's head as she looked at Dora. Everything matched so perfectly. The smart blue suit with its pink paisley trim. The little shoes. The hair backcombed to perfection.

'What Follows has come very close, Dee. He mustn't find us yet.'

Eddie was talking quietly to Dora, who sat at her painted tea, her rosebud lips pursed in a meaningless and permanent pout. Her hair was so clever, it took the baby roundness out of her face, and somehow all the rosiness had gone. Her face was pale – even the lips were white rose now.

Those white lips …

'It's HER fault. She brought It to us.' Dora was standing up and pointing. Edward was shushing her.

'Dee, you can't stay here anyway. Didn't you look at that last consignment of beds? And haven't you noticed what you're wearing?'

Good old Teddy. That caught her attention.

'What I'm wearing? Just because I'm the first to wear hotpants in the whole store.'

She went to pat approvingly at her legs, looked puzzled, then paled. She whirled accusingly at Em, pointing. 'SHE must have gone back!'

Em couldn't help noticing that she wasn't as angry as she had been about the mustard wool though.

'How could we have found her otherwise, Dee?' pleaded Teddy.

But it seemed obvious that Dorabella didn't mind whether they found her or not. Her clothes were puzzling her, and she was staring at her face in the mirror.

'I did do it well though, didn't I?' She patted smugly at her beehive hair, busily whitening her lips and darkening her eyes.

'Dee, we can't stay. Just go and say you have to leave early. It's nearly closing time anyway.' Patient old Teddy. How coaxing he was.

'Closing Time!' Em realised what he had said. 'Ted, you mean the end of her shift don't you.'

Ted's button eye looked into hers and she knew he meant Closing Time. Though she had known it anyway when she had seen they couldn't get back from the Staff Canteen.

'We have to go, Dee. Now.' He gave a furry paw to each of them and they began to walk towards the kitchen doors. The only doors now – suppose they had waited – suppose Ted hadn't been with them … Through the swing doors they went, hands linked, through the doors which had been disgorging Waiters, with tray upon tray of plastic delights.

Em was not surprised to find no bustling kitchen, no Cookers, not even a plastics factory. Instead they stood in a high vaulted tunnel where columns of red marble and sparkling granite soared and arched above them.

'Teddy, did … is this what we made?'

'Yes. This is part of the Beginning.'

The beginning.

'Teddy – Edward Bear – tell me, straight out, is there a chance we could all get home?'

'All get home?' Edward echoed her, on a question. And he stressed the 'all'.

Em's heart seemed to drop. We aren't all here! How long have you been looking for me, Ted? And who else …?

'Hurry, Emily, Dee. We have a train to catch.'

Hand in hand they walked down the vaulted marble halls – and now Em knew where she was! This was the underground railway system that would rival Moscow's for grandeur and beauty. This was Central. In time it was planned that it would link with the furthest outposts of the world. It had spread way beyond the utopian dreams of its designers.

'I've got food. And water. From the canteen,' said Ted.

He handed them each water bottles and packets.

'But Ted. They'll feed us on the train, won't they?'

The trains were to be like the Orient Express in its heyday. And everything First Class. Everyone deserves first class, Papa had said. Well that was the plan. Now … Edward was right, as usual. It would be a long, long journey. And water only seemed to come in bottles. What had the Cleaners been using, she wondered vaguely.

Perhaps floors didn't get very dirty, now there were no Shoppers to tread on them.

But all that was fading and a lot of things were coming back to her. You wouldn't have needed provisions to get from Central to Greystones at one time. It was a short journey then.

'Edward, when did we lose each other?' Em stopped, because it seemed to her that in the dim distant past, which was also the future, it was she who had left them. How long had they been trying to reach her, before she turned back and found them? But they came to the platform before she could catch and hold the thought.

It was a horror. It was dark and shadowy. And vast. Now populations of Cities could have waited here. Ted pulled them briskly along, making no attempt to answer Em's gabbled questions. He was rushing them down to the left, away from the dark depths, where, vaguely in the distance Em could see a group of … passengers …?

Passengers … but if they were passengers, weren't they also Shoppers?

She felt a chill of horror run down to her toes. They must be warned. Maybe they could get near enough to shout. 'Ted.' It was hard to get her breath, her legs now too short to keep up with Teddy's sturdy ones. 'Ted, Shoppers ahead, I saw … they got hold of him, two of them … one on each side.'

'It's OK' said the voice of Edward Bear. 'They are Passengerpersons.'

'Passengerpersons. But Eddie, why would they make Passengerpersons. What would they be for …?' Em's voice tailed off as she noticed that Dorabella was looking at her scornfully.

So – it should be obvious what they were for. When the mechanism began to take itself over, as planned, it had produced such wonderful things for them – the Cleaners, the Sellers, the Waiters, the Watchers. Their lives had become a dream of lotus-eating. Even she, Em, lost without credit had … Well, what had she been doing? And how long ago was it?

She had slept on the most sumptuous beds, in gorgeous bedding. No-one had disturbed her after lightset. Just an occasional Watcher had wheeled round, benevolently flashing a torch. Protecting her.

But then – when? – the closures had started. There had been the Coffee Shop, with its vast free buffet. How long had she lived there, on that plush sofa on the foyer? Watching the gorgeous crowds come and go. Things were disappearing and dissolving as she tried to think about them. But, one day, it hadn't opened. Or had the foyer got so big she simply couldn't find it anymore?

She'd had to move on. Whole malls were closing. Bazaar upon bazaar didn't open. The deadness had started.

Shoppers had begun to decrease. But that was a line of thought best not followed. That Street … the Last Shopper, lost in his dream of consuming, and the gleam in the eyes of the Two Carpetsellers.

The Bedseller's eyes had gleamed. But the Mechanism was their friend. It had always protected her.

'Stand here. NO! Not near the edge. We must get on board. It's the last train.'

Once again, Edward was pulling them through. Dorabella was consumed with sulking maliciously over her clothes, which seemed to be getting less and less fashionable every moment. Poor Dorabella. With her chubby face, rosy cheeks and fat little legs, she had been manufactured too soon. She should have been a Barbie.

The Passengerpersons were a slow remorseless incoming tide flowing towards them. She remembered, with a shudder, what Teddy had said about staying away from the edge of the platform

Turning to him, Em asked again what they were for, but her words were drowned by a tremendous roar, as the ground shook and the last train began its approach to the station.

'Hurry, hurry.' Edward was rushing them on. The tide was so close now that Em could see their eyes. And she had seen those eyes before. Slowly they had pulled the Shopper towards their booths – the right booth and the left booth. One on each side – until he woke from his dream of having and began to scream. But they hadn't stopped.

After a while the screaming had stopped.

Now they began to climb the steps to the carriages, Teddy pushing Dorabella ahead of him, pulling Em behind him, panic communicating itself through his furry paws. You could see the whites of their eyes, thought Em, riveted by the robotic tide approaching them. But not feel their hot breath. She wanted to laugh and laugh and never stop.

And where were the Teeth in the darkness? The following Grin? She looked back, over the heads of the passenger tide. Looked right at a scrap of pink, sitting forlornly on a bench.

'Peter Pink! It's Peter.' How could she have forgotten him?

Edward's little brother. That was who they were waiting for. But he wasn't on the train. He was opposite them, right behind the tide of passengers.

Now she must do something. Edward's eye was towards the carriage, scanning anxiously. She pulled away from his paw, ran through the narrow gap left between the train and the Persons. 'It's Peter! He's not on the train!'

'NO. NO. Come back, Emily. Come back.' Or was he shouting, Go back?

'Peter!' Emily panted up to the seat, and reached out her arms. But suddenly Peter turned. And she saw the eyes. Feral, red, they gleamed at her. Greedily.

'I want to eat you for supper, my dear. I want to eat everything for supper.' The pink paws reached out. And behind she heard the train begin to pull out of the station.

Come back, Edward had shouted. Or was it Go back? Back to all the horrors she had come through, back to the dying Mechanism and the teeth in the dark.

No. But there was nowhere else to go. The last train had gone. Emily did the only thing she could. She ran to the platform edge, threw herself off, and ran into the tunnel after the last train.

She ran, stumbling on tracks, crunching on gravel, until finally she gave up and slumped against the side of the tunnel. She couldn't hear anything, except her own breathing. But the pink thing on the bench could come so quietly if it wanted to. Now she was in the darkness, waiting for its teeth to materialise beside her neck, after all Edward's attempts to save her!

The big teeth had grinned their half moon grin and rocked at her. They wanted her. Only her. They didn't want to eat the universe.

The Pink eyes had gleamed. No grin. Just a lust to eat everything there was. Nothing personal, little Emily.

She got up quickly. She would not give up, whatever was following her. But already the track had gone. She started to run. Horrible to run in the darkness, but the gravel was smooth and clear under her feet. She knew it could take months to get to the next station. But home lay somewhere down this tunnel and every step took her nearer to it.

The noise of the gravel under her feet seemed to get louder and louder, drowning out her panting breaths. But her feet were registering No More Gravel.

No more gravel. And in the silence, the sound of things crunching on gravel. No good looking back. And only darkness up ahead.

What was coming now? Not a train. Hold on to that thought. Edward had said The Last Train, and she had seen it go. Not the feral pink imitation – light as silkwater it would make no sound at all. It had seemed for one moment, as she looked into its eyes, she had seen the spirit of the Mechanism.

It could use anything to stop her going home. The Teeth that smiled out of darkness were quiet enough too. A rustle – a faint rocking – almost as if it flew. This noise was like a train – coming at her through the dark, where no train could be.

An auditory illusion? Don't panic, Emily.

Oh No. The realisation caught at her throat. This must be the Passengerthings surging after her. That was what they were for after all. To make sure she did not catch that Last Train. That's why the feral pink Peter didn't bother to follow her. It knew they would come – slow and relentless. They would never get tired. Anymore than the sea did.

The Mechanism was not her friend. Even though they had made it.

'AAAAGGHHH–!' Em's scream was muffled, cut off by the furry paw that had caused it.

'We pulled the cord, and came back for you, little Emily. I said we would.'

So that was what he had been shouting. Hold on, we'll come back.

'We've got to get straight back. Find the track. And go where it takes us.'

'But, Teddy, it's gone. Even the gravel.'

'No, it's there. The death hasn't got here yet. We have to go back to find where it twisted. It will go straight home.'

'No, but Ted, they are coming after us, those Passenger things.'

'They only have one pace. But we have to be quick. Come on. I've got a torch, but we must be careful how we use it.'

How wonderfully resourceful Teddy was. Always was. Why ever did I leave him? A torch flashed briefly, glinting down the tunnel behind them, which was empty, bare earth, just a rumbling on gravel filling the far distance. It glinted briefly on green and then the darkness surged back.

'Oh, Dorabella. Your uniform! It's lovely.' Mama had made the little green tunic for Dora, during Emily's first year at school. Fortunately, Dorabella was too busy rolling up the waistband, and doing mysterious but fashionable things with the sleeves, to hear Em's exclamation.

They moved as quickly as they could back down the tunnel, Edward's torch flashing briefly in darkness. Questions were forming in Emily's head faster than she could ask them. 'Teddy, Peter, that wasn't Peter. Where is he?'

'I know. I know what that was. Peter wasn't on the train, so he'll be waiting in the tunnel. As long as we get to him before …' Edward's torch flashed again quickly, illuminating the tunnel ahead of them. Ahead was darkness. And doors.

'We have to go straight there. As the train was going.' For the first time his voice betrayed uncertainty. Em didn't dare ask the questions forming in her head.

The Mechanism was trying to push her somewhere. But where? Away from Teddy and Dorabella and Peter Pink. And they didn't have Peter Pink.

What had Edward said? Something mustn't happen until they were together?

It was so hard to remember things. It was definitely trying to stop her going home. Why?

It had taken the tracks from under her feet. No. It hadn't. For the first time, she began to glimpse what was happening behind … behind what? It hadn't removed the train lines, it had twisted the tunnel. They would have to go back and find the lines – and then follow them. Home.

Edward said the tracks led home. The Mechanism could not be her friend it if tried to stop her going there. Could not. Believe it and remember it.

'He must be waiting in the tunnel.' Edward's torch flashed again, and now it illuminated row upon row of cubby holes in the tunnel wall. Each one a refuge from any passing train, and each one containing an identical dusty wooden door. Emily didn't like the look of them one bit. Of course, Peter Pink would have hidden in one of these as the train roared past.

'But look, Ted, there are doors in every one. If he's gone through …' Emily's voice tailed off forlornly.

'If he's gone through! No. He won't go through. There is only one door we can go through now.'

'Which door? How will I know it?'

'Shh. It can always hear us. Be very careful.'

Edward's torch flashed down the tunnel – now there was door upon door in the cubby holes on each side. How many doors were there in the world? But these doors all seemed to be the same. Normal sized, wooden, drab and sturdy.

Why so many identical doors just here?

'We must check each one.' With a martyred air, Dorabella took the right hand side, little Emily the left.

Ted's torch shone and glittered, now it illuminated a door, now it shone anxiously down the long tunnel looking for signs of track, while all the time, the roaring and crunching grew louder.

'Hurry, Hurry, Come on Dee! Emily!'

'Wait, look here.' Emily stepped up to the door. She had seen a tiny fluff of pink fur, illuminated for a fraction of a second by Edward's torch. The real Peter Pink had sheltered here. Em grabbed at the soft piece of pink wool and her hand clicked against something. Suddenly the door swung round like the secret door in innumerable childhood stories.

It swung her onto a bright sea shore. She was outside. After how many years enmalled?

She was on a narrow esplanade, beyond which lay all the waters in the world. Unbottled, they roared and surged in joy. So this was where all the water had been going. The Mechanism was creating a seaside so big that there wasn't a word big enough to describe it.

Happy seaside days! Her parents came back vividly to her mind, so happy to have survived the war that had made the Mechanism necessary. The war that had left bomb sites for Emily to play on. And sparklers on the sand. 'Don't touch anything on the beach, little Emily,' Mama had said sternly. 'Don't touch anything.'

And now the Mechanism had made her a safe beach. With no sand.

Perhaps all it had wanted was to bring her here? Maybe everyone else was here too. She looked along the narrow esplanade – which stretched to the horizon to her left and right – uninterrupted by anything.

Sea spray flew up, till Emily's teeth were chattering with the cold. It was exhilarating. She wanted to run and jump, and breathe the air. She could taste water and salt. And something else. Something bitter?

No. She was out here, in the open air. Nothing could follow her here. The seaside was a place full of happiness. Any minute now, Papa and Mama would come into view, hand in hand, happy again. And everything would be alright.

Emily shaded her eyes, stepped forward, looked out to the far, far horizon. And then she saw it.

Words locked and froze in her head, and her eyes blanked. Then slowly the golden paving came up and hit her in the face.

* * *

Gold and cold. Cold and gold. They were two words. And Emily. Another word. Emily is gold and cold. Nonsense. Why did the word Nonsense strike a sharp note of deadly danger?

Gold is pressing coldly on my face. It's hard and cold and gold. But there's something soft and furry under me. Oh, and pink.

Pink for danger! No. That was Red.

101

Little Emily,
Never Tread,
Upon the Road,
When Lights are Red!

The mechanism sang that song. NO. That was Papa. He sang it. That was before the Mechanism. Who needed cars when they had their lovely Mechanism? It had carried them smoothly off through its doors, to wherever they wanted to go.

The Mechanism sang: Never Ever Go Back. What Follows Will catch…

Did that mean, could that mean …? What did Teddy say? It mustn't catch us yet? YET. Not till we are all together. Not till we have found Peter Pink. But that brought a new question. An urgent one. Why am I lying on Peter Pink? I'm squashing him.

I must have fallen over him. He must have been right under my feet all the time. Just as I was seeing … Here Emily's brain hit a blank and burnt out spot.

She knelt up and lifted Peter gently. He was pink and limp, his eyes staring blankly into Nothing.

He has seen Nothing, thought Emily. Nothing.

And I, who got just one glimpse of the Nothingness that is surging along behind all the waters in the world have now got a strange gap in my head. Because I have seen what cannot be seen. And I must never turn round again. I must Go Back, through that door.

Clutching Peter to her, Emily stared at a vast wall of doors stretching as far as the eye could see, all the same, all drab and normal sized. But that didn't matter. She hadn't moved a step from her door, the one that swung her through. Neither had Peter. He had seen Nothing and stayed there doing Nothing ever since. They could go straight back, to Edward and Dorabella.

All the waters in the world surged seductively behind her. Oh the memories we hold for you little Emily. Just one more look.

Oh no, Mechanism, you don't fool me anymore. I've seen where you are taking us. 'Touch nothing, little Emily. Touch Nothing.' That was Mama's voice.

Emily hesitated, and suddenly the doors in front of her began to rock. Then they began to move, as if they were on an endless conveyor. She watched, fascinated, horrified, as a conveyor belt containing all the doors there ever could have been began to rush madly past her, so fast that in the end they were a dizzying, whirling blur.

If you won't move, said the Mechanism, I will move the doors. Now try to go back. She held Peter even tighter. He could do Nothing now.

What follows will catch? Think, Emily. Think while you can.

What was following her? What had rustled in bushes, creaked on stairs, and once had gleamed white teeth at her out of the darkness?

To go back to that?

Impossible.

But to go forward was impossible. And to turn round couldn't even be thought of. Horror in front of her. Horror behind her. No wonder the Mechanism was dying. The mad lust to eat everything she had seen in the eyes of the pink thing, and more obliquely in the eyes of Shoppers, had led them to this. For one fraction of a second, she had seen Nothing.

The mad, whirling, conveyor belt of doors was starting to slow. It was going to stop again. She braced herself. Whatever happened, she must not look behind her. Suddenly the mechanism creaked to a stop, and silenced.

The soft lapping of all the waters in the world called seductively behind her. Mama's and Papa's pleading voices mingling with seagulls' cries. Then right in front of her was a giant's door. A door like this must have opened to Jack after he had climbed his beanstalk. Please don't open to me. I don't want to see what lies behind that door.

But I can't move one inch backwards. And, whatever comes out of that door, Whatever, I must not turn round. I must never look back.

Didn't the walls warn me? They were my friend. No. They are not your friend, Emily. Why can't you remember that? They kept you asleep, in a dream of lotus-eating. And one by one the Shoppers themselves were consumed. Then they drove you to the deadness, away from your home. Away from your friends! The only ones who could help. They tried to stop you going back.

But if they don't want me to go back, then I should Go Back! It was a revelation. But too late. The door back had whirled away forever. Even if I could safely sit here for eons until the door I came through whirled back, I wouldn't recognise it. It had made thousands upon thousands of that deceitful swinging door.

It must have been the only cubby hole when Peter was waiting in the tunnel. That's why he hid in it! Then it made the others, so we would never find him.

How blind I have been. And for how long?

At least I have found Peter. Our real, true Peter Pink. But I've lost the others.

What would they do? Teddy said he had stopped the train by pulling the communication cord. So those simple things still worked. And, if they still worked, was the train waiting there for them? Could they have caught it, and be on their way home?

She clutched Peter tighter, because the mad conveyor belt of doors was beginning to shake. Something was going to happen.

They were going to move again. The shaking increased, as if the doors were revving up, and suddenly a crack appeared in the door in front of her. Something had been shaken loose by the rattling.

A cat flap swinging open? For a giant's cat! Don't step back. Don't look back.

But it was a door. It was the door to 5 Disraeli Crescent. The basement door. The door into the dark stone cellar, the door to the cellar steps with safety at their top.

It was a cat's flap in that giant's door, but normal size. Invitingly open.

The revving increased. She had only seconds to make up her mind. Not that there was a choice really. What was behind her was more terrible than teeth in the dark. And to go through this door really would be going back. It was the door she had been looking for from the first. The one door into home that was never locked.

Em could no longer formulate: 'If it's a trap, it's a clever one'; and, as the revving took off, plunged straight through the door, clutching the inert pink bundle.

Light filtered into the basement room, through the window behind her. Daddy's garden, it was Daddy's garden behind her. She only just stopped herself turning round and running back out. She could not turn round. Behind that door and window … Nothing.

That was the trap. She could see it clear and sharp now. Turn round Emily. You are in your daddy's cellar. Don't go into the darkness. Turn round, to the garden. And daylight.

But if she turned round, she would see Nothing. And she would never see anything again. She would see what was coming very very fast along the horizon of all the water that had ever been. If she hadn't tripped over Peter Pink just as she looked to the horizon …

What had they done? How could they have eaten everything?

Never Look Back. That's what the walls would say now, if they were her friend. Only these were not talking walls. They were the friendly cellar walls of home, flaking plaster dimly seen in faint light from the 'garden' behind her.

She must get to Mama and Papa. They could sort it all out. She must go on through the second cellar. Yes, it was the same. Almost completely dark. And there was the white stone table gleaming at her. White as teeth. Don't … remember, even the Teeth are better than Nothing.

Hysterical giggling won't help either, Emily told herself as sternly as she could.

Tiptoe through, past the darkest of darkness, the cellar within the cellar that leads who knows where, clutching Peter Pink so tightly. She had never been down into that dark place, that area under the cellar stairs. And even with her slightly burnt brain, touched by Nothing, she would not be so foolish as to do so now.

Little Emily
Have a look
At your goose
For it is cooked!

Had Papa been chalking nursery rhymes on the cellar walls? Or was the Mechanism right here, in the cellar with her? She looked fearfully down into the depth of darkness under the stairs. She couldn't see Nothing. But was there a faint gleam way off in the distance? Faint sounds of gravel? How long was that darkness now?

But it couldn't hold her back. She was at the cellar steps. Hold on Peter Pink. Mama and Papa are at the top. But the cellar steps looked so big. So steep and high. The white stone gleamed at the bottom and disappeared into darkness at the top. And she could hear waters beginning to creep under the garden door behind her, through two cellar rooms. She would never get up those stairs quickly enough. Already she felt as if she were wading through treacle, and Peter was getting so big and heavy in her arms.

Without any warning, something else gleamed and smiled beside her. A set of white teeth, rocking in the darkness.

Peter Pink was pulled from her numb arms. She let him go without resistance.

'Get up, Emily. Quick!'

Edward. How could Edward be here? Furry paws pulled and heaved at her.

She was pulled past the teeth, grinning and gleaming in the dark cellar and found herself sitting astride a saddle – Dora in front of her, Edward behind her.

It was Dobbin. It was Dobbin's smile. His teeth that had

grinned at her in the dead area. It was Dobbin who had creaked on the stairs above her. He had come after her too! Rocking tenaciously along, through the darkness and the deadness.

'Hurry, Dee. Emily's got Peter Pink. She's got him safe.'

And now Dobbin began to gallop. To race to beat the tide of Nothingness that would soon be lapping at the foot of the cellar steps.

No. Not lapping. It would be doing Nothing at the foot of the cellar steps.

Up the steps they flew. Dobbin's mane streaming in the wind. Edward clutching Emily, who clutched Peter Pink, who slumped behind Dorabella at the reins. Dora was wearing a very smart pair of jodhpurs that Emily didn't remember at all, but Dobbin ignored all her attempts to ride in a dressage manner, and just kept flying.

Up and up and up they galloped. Emily relaxed. Dobbin would do it now, Nothing wouldn't stop him. He would get them back to Papa and Mama and then they would be safe.

He was set for home, once he had found a rider. Dobbin could outrun anything. Faster than the wind he was. And that's why they couldn't let him find them until they were all together. How awful if it had just been the three of them and Peter Pink still sitting on that fatal shore. There was no need for her to struggle and run anymore. Her eyes closed.

You came back for me. You all came back for me. And we've got home, Emily thought, a feeling of joy and safety flooding over her. Papa and Mama would sort everything out.

The room was warm and sleepy; firelight flickering into the dark corners, illuminating Daddy and the men from the office. Lighting up Uncle Ted Danby's glasses, picking out blue numbers on the arm of Uncle Jan Rosenfeldt.

'They have to do it, Jan.' That was Uncle Ted's gruff voice. 'We can't have any more of these dreadful wars.'

'It's the power source.' Papa and Uncle Jan's voices were worried, but willing to be persuaded. 'They can't quantify the amount of power it's going to generate.'

'But the way they've designed it, the whole mechanism is going to sort that out for us, that's the beauty of it.'

'It's like tapping into the power of the Universe! And we'll be part of the beginning. Us, right here, in our city.' They could not resist.

How their eyes shone in the firelight.

Fragments of memory caught and held for a moment before they flew away into the fire. The Mechanism. How nice it sounded.

The Sellers' eyes had shone. There had been a pulling. And a screaming, turning into a red silence.

'Papa. Papa. It isn't …'

It isn't … You shouldn't … don't … What? The fire roared, and soothed.

'Yes it is, young Miss, in fact it's well past your bedtime. Mama! Mama! It's past Emmie's bedtime. She's falling asleep on her rocking horse.'

Papa came over. He was so tall, and so young. He lifted her gently into the big sofa by the fire. 'Finish your milk, Emmy, and Mama will take you to bed.'

Emily looked at her companions for help. They were all there, all present and correct. Dobbin was rocking gently, his big white teeth grinning in the firelight. Peter Pink was slumped in her lap, staring vacantly into Nothing. Edward Bear sprawled on the sofa, his button turned to the fire. And beside him was rosy-cheeked Dorabella, sulking silently in mustard-coloured wool.

Publisher's note: *Till They Dropped* was first published by Fantastic Books Publishing as a standalone novella. It is also available as an audio book.

About the Author

Sue Knight writes novels, short stories and poems. Much of her work has been inspired by childhood memories, her 20 years living in the Middle East, and her many trips to the Maldive Islands.

Sue publishes a blog regularly
at https://sueknight2000.blogspot.com/

Also by Sue Knight

Novels & novellas
Till They Dropped
Waiting for Gordo
Disraeli Hall

Poetry
Old Playgrounds
Sue was an invited contributor to the poetry anthology, Ours.

If you have enjoyed this book, please consider leaving a review on Amazon and Goodreads for Sue Knight to let her know what you thought of her work.

Printed in Great Britain
by Amazon

47153371R10069